One Hot RUMOR

Other Books by Anna Durand

Lachlan in a Kilt (The Ballachulish Trilogy, Book One)
Aidan in a Kilt (The Ballachulish Trilogy, Book Two)
Rory in a Kilt (The Ballachulish Trilogy, Book Three)
The American Wives Club (A Hot Brits/Hot Scots/Au Naturel Crossover)
Brit vs. Scot (A Hot Brits/Hot Scots/Au Naturel Crossover)
Dangerous in a Kilt (Hot Scots, Book One)
Wicked in a Kilt (Hot Scots, Book Two)
Scandalous in a Kilt (Hot Scots, Book Three)
The MacTaggart Brothers Trilogy (Hot Scots, Books 1-3)
Gift-Wrapped in a Kilt (Hot Scots, Book Four)
Notorious in a Kilt (Hot Scots, Book Five)
Insatiable in a Kilt (Hot Scots, Book Six)
Lethal in a Kilt (Hot Scots, Book Seven)
Irresistible in a Kilt (Hot Scots, Book Eight)
Devastating in a Kilt (Hot Scots, Book Nine)
Spellbound in a Kilt (Hot Scots, Book Ten)
Relentless in a Kilt (Hot Scots, Book Eleven)
The Notorious Dr. MacT (A Hot Scots Prequel)
The British Bastard (A Hot Scots Prequel)
One Hot Chance (Hot Brits, Book One)
One Hot Roomie (Hot Brits, Book Two)
One Hot Crush (Hot Brits, Book Three)
The Dixon Brothers Trilogy (Hot Brits, Books 1-3)
One Hot Escape (Hot Brits, Book Four)
One Hot Christmas (Hot Brits, Book Six)
One Hot Scandal (Hot Brits, Book Seven)
Natural Passion (Au Naturel Trilogy, Book One)
Natural Impulse (Au Naturel Trilogy, Book Two)
Natural Satisfaction (Au Naturel Trilogy, Book Three)
Echo Power (Echo Power Trilogy, Book One)
Echo Dominion (Echo Power Trilogy, Book Two)
Echo Unbound (Echo Power Trilogy, Book Three)
The Mortal Falls (Undercover Elementals, Book One)
The Mortal Fires (Undercover Elementals, Book Two)
The Mortal Tempest (Undercover Elementals, Book Three)
The Janusite Trilogy (Undercover Elementals, Books 1-3)
Obsidian Hunger (Undercover Elementals, Book Four)
Unbidden Hunger (Undercover Elementals, Book Five)
The Thirteenth Fae (Undercover Elementals, Book Six)
Willpower (Psychic Crossroads, Book One)
Intuition (Psychic Crossroads, Book Two)
Kinetic (Psychic Crossroads, Book Three)
Passion Never Dies: The Complete Reborn Series

One Hot RUMOR

Hot Brits, Book Five

ANNA DURAND

JACOBSVILLE BOOKS · JB · MARIETTA, OHIO`

ONE HOT RUMOR

ISBN: 978-1-949406-55-9 (paperback)
ISBN: 978-1-949406-56-6 (ebook)
ISBN: 978-1-949406-57-3 (audiobook)

Manufactured in the United States.

Jacobsville Books
www.JacobsvilleBooks.com

Publisher's Cataloging-in-Publication Data
provided by Five Rainbows Cataloging Services

Names: Durand, Anna.
Title: One hot rumor / Anna Durand.
Description: Marietta, OH : Jacobsville Books, 2021. | Series: Hot Brits, bk. 5.
Identifiers: ISBN 978-1-949406-55-9 (paperback) | ISBN 978-1-949406-56-6
   (ebook) | ISBN 978-1-949406-57-3 (audiobook)
Subjects: LCSH: Rumor--Fiction. | Scandals--Fiction. | Masseurs--Fiction. |
   Adult college students--Fiction. | British--Fiction. | Romance fiction. | BISAC:
   FICTION / Romance / Contemporary. | FICTION / Romance / Romantic
   Comedy. | FICTION / Romance / Later in Life. | GSAFD: Love stories.
Classification: LCC PS3604.U724 O56 2020 (print) | LCC PS3604.U724 (ebook) |
   DDC 813/.6--dc23.

Chapter One

Nick

I never meant to become the center of a scandal, but one disgruntled client started a rumor that spread like wildfire. Now everyone in my hometown thinks I'm the sort of man who gives "special" massages at my day spa. I'm a massage therapist, not a gigolo, but no one cares about that. Apparently, I've become a "meme" on social media, whatever that means. I needed to get away for a while until the fire snuffs out. Hunkering down in my house only worked until someone found my address, hiding out at my parents' house got bloody boring after three weeks, and my brother's suggestion that I take a holiday for a few weeks didn't appeal to me either. I decided to do something different.

Go back to school. Finish my university degree. And do it in America.

Why? Because it's far away from England and the scandal that's threatening to ruin my career. My right-hand man, Bennett Montague, can handle things while I'm gone.

So here I am walking into a building called Rathbone Hall at a school called Vallefrio University in northern New Mexico. The desert is a new experience for me, but this morning, I have other things on my mind. I'm to meet my faculty adviser, someone called Dr. SJ Griffin, Professor of Mathematics. That's what it says on the bloke's door, anyway. I read those words as I walk through the open door of the office.

A young woman sits at a desk holding a phone to her ear.

When she notices me, she holds up a finger in the universal gesture that means "keep quiet, you arse, I'm busy."

"No, Jimmy," she tells the caller, "I can't cut out early to go to the liquor store and get your loser friends a twenty-four-pack of beer. Get it yourself. We're not dating anymore, which means I'm not your beer slave. Goodbye."

She scowls as she punches her mobile screen to disconnect the call.

"Good morning," I say, smiling. "I have an appointment with Dr. SJ Griffin."

The girl brushes red hair away from her eyes. "Oh right, you're the new…" Her gaze wanders over me, and she bites one side of her bottom lip. "Uh, are you sure you're in the right place? Dr. Griffin's nine o'clock appointment is supposed to be with a new student."

"That's me." But I know I don't look like a student. I'm nineteen years older than when I gave up on my degree, so I can't blame the girl for being confused. "I'm Nick Hunter. Dr. Griffin is expecting me, and yes, I am a new student."

"But you're British and middle-aged."

Middle-aged? I may not be a teenager, but bloody hell, do I look middle-aged?

The girl winces. "Sorry. That came out wrong. It's just that you're, um, older than most of our students. I'm Lana, by the way, Dr. Griffin's graduate assistant. You can wait in here. It should just be a few minutes."

"May I sit down?"

"Yeah, go ahead."

"Thank you, Lana."

She walks out of the office, leaving the door open.

I amble past the desk she vacated, one that clearly belongs to a professor. It has pens and pencils in a coffee mug, a desk calendar with notes scrawled on it, and various math-related things like a protractor and a scientific calculator. Oddly, there's no computer. But there is a lamp and a stack of books with mathy titles.

Wonderful. My adviser is probably an elderly gent who wears bifocals and sniffles all the time.

Two chairs sit in front of the desk, so I settle onto one and prop my feet on the desk's corner. If I have to wait for my crotchety adviser, I might as well get comfortable. Slouching in my chair, I lean my head against its back and close my eyes. The long flight from the UK has left me knackered.

"Ahem," someone says. "Would you mind getting your big feet off my desk?"

That's not a crotchety gent's voice.

I open my eyes—and sit up straighter, pulling my feet off the desk.

The woman standing in the doorway has raven hair and amber eyes, not to mention skin so smooth and creamy that it's like fine alabaster. Her lips are puckered, probably because she's annoyed with me. A tweed skirt suit molds to her body, highlighting her sensual figure, but it still manages to be professional. She's tied her hair up in a bun, and even that makes me hot for her, especially the way a few locks have fallen over her ears.

Well, maybe Dr. SJ Griffin isn't so bad after all.

She takes a seat behind her desk and brings a laptop computer out of the bag she had carried over her shoulder. Setting the laptop to one side, she rolls her chair forward and folds her arms on the desktop. "You're Nicholas Hunter, I presume. Welcome to Vallefrio University. I'm your faculty adviser, Dr. SJ Griffin."

"I know. And you can call me Nick."

"No, Mr. Hunter, I will not be doing that."

"But I prefer it. We don't need to be so formal, do we? I'm not an eighteen-year-old freshman."

She scans me up and down, her lips puckering again. "Yes, you're awfully old to be a student."

Why does everyone keep saying that? And why do I feel the need to defend myself?

No idea, but my mouth has its own logic. "My great uncle went to university for the first time five years ago. He was seventy-nine."

"Mm-hm." Dr. SJ Griffin pulls a file folder out of her bag and spreads it open on the desktop, then she slips on a pair of reading glasses and focuses on the papers in the folder. "Nicholas Hunter, forty years old, a foreign student with transfer credits from the University of Reading."

"I'm impressed. You pronounced the name correctly. How did you know it's Redding and not Reeding?"

She glances at me briefly but doesn't answer my question, then returns to studying her dossier on me. "I see you had an adequate GPA."

Adequate? I don't care how sexy she is, this woman is too uptight to be any fun. "Do I get to know everything about you too?"

"No." She gnaws on her lip like a rabbit chewing on a carrot and tugs on her earlobe, which I find adorable until she speaks again. "Only freshmen get faculty advisers, but someone pulled a lot of strings on your behalf. Don't expect special treatment because you've got connections. Your advanced age does not grant you any favors."

"That would be my brother, Richard. He pulled those strings, I mean. But I expect to work my arse off like any other college student." I smirk. "Despite my advanced age."

She chews on her lip again, rabbit-style, then shuts her eyes and sighs. When she looks at me, her expression softens—a little. "I think we've gotten off on the wrong foot, Mr. Hunter."

"Yes, I agree. Not sure why, but I feel like it's somehow my fault."

"It's not you." She sits up ramrod straight and tugs her jacket down as if it needs straightening, though it doesn't. "I apologize for my rudeness."

"No worries. I've heard much worse lately, and I realize my age is a bit of a surprise."

"That's no excuse for my behavior." She glances at her file folder, head down, then looks at me from under her beautiful lashes. "I know who you are, Mr. Hunter. Your age and your connections made me curious, and I, um, looked you up online."

She can't know about my recent troubles. There must thousands of Nick Hunters online.

"Your home address is in your file," she says, sounding almost embarrassed. "So I didn't have much trouble finding you."

Oh bugger. She must've read all about my scandal. No wonder she's treating me like a criminal.

"Let me explain," I say. "Whatever you've read is not the truth. It's a rumor, one that does not reflect who I am or what my business is about. I'm a massage therapist, and I own a day spa in Cockshire. It's not where I was born, but I've lived there for years."

Her lips tighten, but it seems more like humor this time. "Cockshire? You're pulling my leg. That's too on the nose for you."

"Is it my fault somebody called the town Cockshire? It's spelled S-H-I-R-E, by the way, not S-U-R-E."

My sexy adviser leans back in her chair, her lips curving upward just enough to give me hope she's not as uptight as she seems. "Did you move there because of the name? It describes you so well, and you seem like the type who loves double entendres."

"I do, but that has no bearing on why I moved to that town."

"Why, then?"

Because I didn't want to be just Richard Hunter's brother who runs a massage business. Moving to a neighboring town kept me close to my family without Rick's shadow hanging over me all the time. It sounds narcissistic, though, and I don't care to admit the truth to SJ Griffin. So I change the subject.

"What's your first name?" I ask. "Calling you SJ will be awkward."

"You will call me Dr. Griffin. Maintaining appropriate boundaries is essential in a teacher-student relationship."

"Can't we be friends? I don't know anyone in America. Well, except for a few Scots I've gotten to know lately, but they live in Utah."

"You have Scottish friends? All mine are American, except for Sanjay Desai. He's British, like you."

"Are you shagging him?" When she puckers her lips again, I realize I probably shouldn't have blurted that out. "I meant are you, ah, romantically involved with that bloke."

"No, I am not. We're friends. But I know you were asking if I'm screwing him, and I don't appreciate it."

"Sorry. If you're friends with him, why can't you be friends with me?" I raise my hand to stop her when she starts to speak. "I'm not an average student, am I? And I'll gladly sign a waiver granting you my permission to sexually harass me to your pretty little heart's content."

"You're insane."

I shrug. "As you well know, I've been called worse. On the internet. By anonymous wankers who don't have the nerve to say things like that to my face."

"Uh-huh." She closes her file folder. "Why did you quit one semester short of getting your degree in business?"

Somehow, I'd hoped she wouldn't notice that, or at least wouldn't mention it. Of course she noticed and mentioned it. A student of advanced age who quit nineteen years ago within spitting distance of earning that degree? Anyone would be curious.

Dr. Griffin seems more curious than most people.

"It's a long story," I say. "My reasons are personal, and I don't know you. Now, if we had lunch together and chatted to each other, I might feel more comfortable sharing my life story with you."

One corner of her mouth slants upward into a grudging smile. "Are you blackmailing me into having lunch with you?"

"I can't blackmail you since I don't have anything on you." I smile. "Not yet."

Maybe I shouldn't flirt with her, but I can't help it. Underneath her prim exterior, I sense there's a wild woman dying to get out.

SJ Griffin picks up a pen and taps it on her lips. "You're going to give me trouble, aren't you? The university has a code of ethics, one by which I am bound to abide."

"Could you say 'bound to abide' again? It's the sexiest thing I've ever heard."

My luscious adviser stands up, stretching out a hand to offer me a business card. "Here's my office number if you need anything. Please go to the bookstore and buy all your textbooks. Classes begin on Monday."

I get up and take her business card. "Is your home number on the back?"

"No." She sits down. "I saw that you've registered for one of my classes. You won't get any slack just because you're older than the average student. Business analytics is an advanced statistics course. I hope you can handle it."

"You really have low expectations for me, don't you?"

"Realistic expectations. A lot has changed in the past nineteen years." She points at her laptop. "We have computers now."

"Oh yes, we had to make do with parchment scrolls back in the Dark Ages when I was growing up, but I can adapt. Do you have a quill pen I could borrow?"

Her lips twitch, but she doesn't quite smile. "Go buy your books, Mr. Hunter. You're probably staying in the dorms, eh? With all those nubile coeds."

"I have a flat off-campus, for your information." And my brother is paying for it, but I don't need to tell her that. I lean over her desk to gaze straight into her eyes. "If not lunch, then have dinner with me. I need advising. Lots of it. You can't abandon a student from another country who has no idea how to survive in America. And at my advanced age, I might need help finding the right classrooms."

"Sure you will." She eyes me from head to toe like she had when she first saw me. "Why do you want to dress like a frat boy? You're a grown man."

"What's wrong with my clothes?" I'm wearing my Arsenal T-shirt, because I love football, and also stonewashed blue jeans and cowboy boots. Don't Americans love cowboys? Not my adviser, I guess. When I was getting dressed this morning, this outfit seemed appropriate for my first day at university.

Dr. Griffin screws up her mouth, then shrugs. "Goodbye, Mr. Hunter."

Since I've been dismissed, I walk out of her office. Dr. SJ Griffin intrigues me, but I came here to finish my degree, not chat up my faculty adviser. I shouldn't flirt anymore. Kissing her is absolutely out of the question. Under no circumstances will I offer her a "special" massage.

Unless...

No, you sodding arse, you're here to learn, not to seduce SJ Griffin.

Not knowing her first name has made me want her even more. To strip off those stuffy, yet somehow sexy, clothes could be the best time I've had in years. The uptight ones often turn out to be the most incredible lovers once they let go.

But I will not cock up getting my degree. I've waited a long time for this, and I will behave like the mature man I'm supposed to be. All work and no play might drive me barking mad, but I will prove to everyone I am a serious businessman.

I'm halfway to the door that leads out of the building when I realize I've made my first mistake not ten minutes after meeting Dr. Griffin. I hurry back to her office and open the door just enough to poke my head inside. Lana is sitting in the chair where I'd sat a few minutes ago while Dr. Griffin is studying papers on her desk.

"Sorry," I say. "Forgot to ask where the ruddy bookstore is."

Dr. Griffin looks up from her computer, seeming mildly startled. "What?"

"I don't know where the bookstore is."

"Didn't you get a map in your welcome packet?"

"Possibly. But I sort of left that in my flat."

She gives me a teacher-like look of stern disappointment. "Lana can get you another one."

My sexy adviser goes back to studying her computer screen.

I get a map from little Lana and leg it to the bookstore.

Chapter Two

Dr. Griffin

I will never tell Nick Hunter my first name. Dr. Griffin will do just fine because I suspect telling him my first name would lead to lots of flirting and innuendo, not to mention sexy smiles. He'd probably mold my name into dirty syllables simply by speaking it in that steamy British voice. Yes, all right, he's hot. But I do not have sex with students. Not that I was even thinking about that. *Ugh.* Of course I was. How could I not? The man is ridiculously hot, and I'd love to spend one night with him, if only to find out what a "special" massage is. I can't do that, though. I'd lose my job if anyone found out, so I'll stick to fantasizing about Nick Hunter.

He's forty years old and a college senior. Maybe that shouldn't bother me, but it does a little. I'm forty-two, so I can hardly criticize him for his age. Why did I do exactly that? I acted snippy because I'm attracted to him. I've had bad experiences with immature men of a certain age, meaning men over thirty-five. Nick dresses like a frat boy and acts like he doesn't take anything seriously. Sure, those faded blue jeans look sexy on him, and I can't help liking the stubble on his face even though I normally don't like that kind of thing. His cowboy boots give him a strange bad-boy appeal. A Brit wearing western boots? Somehow it works for him.

But I don't get his shirt. It's dark red and has the word ARSENAL printed in capital letters on it under a drawing of what looks like the London skyline.

God, I love his eyes. When he leaned over my desk, I got a good look at those baby blues.

No, I don't love his eyes. He's a student, which means I notice nothing except his GPA.

Ten minutes after Nick Hunter left my office, my cell phone rings while I'm engrossed in creating lesson plans for the summer semester.

I answer my call with my usual greeting since I didn't bother to glance at the caller ID. "Dr. Griffin, professor of mathematics, speaking."

"Jeez, you'll never get a date if you say that to everyone."

"Dating isn't a priority for me."

"No, really?" says the snarky female on the other end of the call. "I know you've been burned before, but come on. You should at least try to get some."

"Sure, I'll 'get some' food at lunch, and I'll 'get some' work done."

"You are so not funny. Getting laid, that's what you need."

I groan. How many times have we had this conversation? No matter how often I explain, she refuses to listen. "Sweetie, please stop encouraging me to have casual sex with random men. It makes me worry about what you're getting up to."

"Did I say anything about random sex with random guys? I want you to find somebody so you won't be alone now that I'm gone."

"You aren't gone," I say, quashing the impulse to snort derisively. "Despite sharing an apartment with Tricia, you turn up at home every other day looking for food or clothes or DVDs."

"Jeez, Mom, DVDs are so last century. But your broadband is better than what we get." She sighs with the kind of long-suffering melodrama only an eighteen-year-old can pull off. "At least answer your phone like you want to talk to people. Please, for me? Please, please, please?"

"I'll try." My lips are curling up at the corners. I can't help it. My daughter always knows how to make me smile. "Was there a reason you called? Because I do have work to do."

"There's a reason." She pauses, then switches to a stage whisper. "I heard there's a new student, and he's a hot British guy."

"He's too old for you, Felicity."

"Is he, like, your age? That's what I heard. I like older guys. Maybe I should ask him out."

"No, absolutely not. Nick Hunter is off-limits for you."

"For me? But not for you, that's what your statement implies." She reverts to her stage whisper. "He must be super-wicked hot if you're warning me away from him. I was kidding about the older-guys thing, but you should go for it. Tap that already."

"I can't express how disturbing it is to hear you sing the praises of casual sex."

"Chill, Mom, I'm still a virgin."

Oh thank God. I don't say that out loud because it would make my daughter laugh hysterically. She thinks I'm uptight. Nick Hunter probably thinks the same thing. Not that I care what he thinks.

There will be absolutely no "'tapping" of anyone.

But his smile…his body…

No, no, no. I'm a mature, professional woman, not a lustful teenager.

At least Felicity hasn't rushed to lose her virginity. She wouldn't lie to me about that or anything. My relationship with my daughter is the best thing in my life, since men only ever let me down. Catastrophically. Somebody should invent disaster insurance for relationships to save me from making another horrible mistake. You know, the kind of insurance that prevents you from doing the walk of shame or crying your eyes out for three days straight.

That idea has nothing whatsoever to do with Nick Hunter.

"Soooo," Felicity says in her sneaky-snarky voice, "you must know the British hottie. Nick Hunter? You wouldn't know his name unless you'd met him. I need the deets, Mom. How finger-lickin' delish is he?"

Good enough to eat him up and go back for seconds.

But I tell Felicity, "I'm his adviser, so yes, I've met him. He's… fine. But don't get excited because I won't see him very often. Faculty advisers are for occasional advising, not daily chats."

Except Nick is taking one of my classes, which means I'll see him four days a week. My tummy flutters when I think about that.

I glare down at my belly. *Stop that, you stupid tummy.*

"Uh-huh," Felicity says. "I bet Nick will need lots of advising. I mean, he is in a foreign country where he doesn't know anybody and doesn't know his way around."

How does she make that sound like I'll be screwing Nick in my office every day? Showing someone around the campus is not a salacious act. Not that I'll be showing him around. Lana gave him a map, so he doesn't need a tour guide.

"When can I meet him?" Felicity asks.

"Nick Hunter? Never, I hope."

She laughs. "Wow, Mom, you're crushing hard on him, aren't you?"

"Don't you have a class to go to?"

"It's summer. I don't start until the end of August." She does that silly whispering thing again. "Is Nick Hunter taking one of your classes?"

"Yes."

"Which one? Because I was thinking about auditing one of your summer classes to, you know, get a jump on my higher education."

"And you think I'm going to tell you which one the 'British hottie' is taking? No way."

"Okay, okay. Don't have an aneurysm. You can have Nick all to yourself."

I hear voices in the background at her end. "Where are you, Felicity?"

"At the mall. I'm meeting Tricia for a marathon shopping spree, and I've got your credit card in my pocket."

"Very funny. Dinner will be at seven, if you're coming home tonight. Don't be late."

"Am I ever? Being late is a crime, being on time is proper, and being early is a virtue. That's number three on the list of the Griffin Rules of Etiquette."

Sure, I've said that. I don't have an actual list, but hearing her recite my rules makes me sound...so uptight.

Maybe I do need to get laid.

"I better go," Felicity says. "Have fun with Nick the Hot Brit. Bye, Mom."

She hangs up before I can complain about what she called Nick.

He might be hot and British, but I am required to adhere to the university's code of ethics. That means no sex with Nick. No kissing Nick. No flirting with Nick. I should probably avoid him as much as possible, and I will not let myself admire his body. If I must speak to him, I'll look him in the eye.

Those gorgeous blue eyes…

I growl at myself and try to focus on the lesson plans I'd been working on before Felicity called to harass me about my lack of male companionship. I don't notice time passing, but suddenly, I realize the clock on my computer says it's one o'clock. In the afternoon. No wonder my tummy had started grumbling a little while ago.

Rising from my chair, I yawn and stretch.

Since the campus cafeteria is the closest place to get food, I make my way out of Rathbone Hall and across the quad. I've just passed the statue of the Spanish explorer Juan de Oñate when someone calls out my name.

"Dr. Griffin, slow down."

Oh God, not *him* again. I stop and turn to face the man who's striding toward me.

Nick Hunter walks with his shoulders back, his spine straight, and his head held high. A slight smile tugs at his lips, and his gaze is aimed straight at me. Naturally, having his attention focused on me makes a tingly warmth chase over my skin.

He halts too close for my comfort, which means less than a continent separates us. "I love the way you walk, like you've urgently got to be somewhere. It's sexy, Dr. Griffin."

I wish he'd stop calling me that. Wish he'd stop talking, period. And stop standing there, looking gorgeous and edible. In fact, it would be perfect if he could just poof out of existence.

"Did you need something?" I ask, and wince because that sounds like an invitation for him to suggest something dirty. "I mean, something related to your education here at Vallefrio."

He moves closer, his body only two feet from mine. "Yes, Dr. Griffin, I desperately need your help. I can't find my way around this campus."

Sure, he's lost and helpless. I'd bet all the money in my savings account that every female who sees him offers to be his campus guide.

"Try Google Maps," I say. "You can zoom in on the campus to see all the streets and buildings. It even tells you the names of those buildings."

"But I need personal attention from my adviser." He glances around like he's afraid someone might overhear what he says next, then he bends his head to within inches of my face. "I've asked a dozen people, and no one can tell me where to get a decent cuppa."

"Maybe because they don't understand what you're asking for."

"A cuppa."

"Which is what, exactly? Americans don't speak British, Mr. Hunter."

He straightens, and one side of his mouth twists upward. "Yes, I'm beginning to realize that. My brother and my mates told me this would happen, but I assumed they were having me on."

"I have no idea what you're talking about."

"My brother and our mates, the Dixons, have all married American women. Well, Richard will marry Maddie in a month, but they're already living together."

Why is he telling me about his friends and family? It doesn't clear up the "cuppa" issue at all.

Nick shoves his hands into his jeans pockets and gives me a sheepish look. "Sorry. I'm babbling, aren't I? 'Cuppa' means a cup of tea. I can't find anyplace on this campus where I can get one of those."

"Try Starbucks. It's a block off campus."

"Which way?" He squints as he scans the surroundings, then he suddenly groans and shuts his eyes. "Bugger me."

"Do what now?"

He looks at me, his shoulders slumping. "I can't remember where I parked my car."

The defeated expression on his face plucks my sympathy strings. I try not to feel bad for him—honestly, I try so hard—but I've always been a sucker for a pathetic, sexy man.

"Come with me," I say. "Let's look for your car."

"Thank you, Dr. Griffin. You're a real mate."

"Uh-huh. Did you have to put coins in a meter, or did you have a student parking card?"

"The former."

"We'll start with the metered lot that's closest to the main campus."

I start walking, waving for him to follow. He falls into step alongside me, walking with that same self-assurance as earlier, and he keeps glancing at me sideways with a faint smirk on his lips. Did he trick me into helping him? No, I don't believe that. He had seemed genuinely upset when he realized he forgot where he parked his car.

But I'm sure he'll now take advantage of the situation to flirt with me.

We reach the first metered parking lot, and it's packed.

"See your car yet?" I ask.

He squints and scans the parking lot, just like he'd scanned the quad a few minutes ago. Then he grins and points to a vehicle three cars away from where we're standing. "There it is. Blimey, I was afraid I'd have to sleep on a park bench tonight."

"You've never heard of taxicabs?"

"I hate those." Nick aims his playful grin at me. "Maybe I could sleep on your couch, Dr. Griffin."

Will he never stop calling me that? Sure, I ordered him to use my professional name, but I hadn't realized how often he would say it or how hot he would sound doing that.

"There are sofas in the administration building," I say. "But you found your car, so you won't need to crash on anybody's furniture."

He takes my hand, lifting it to his lips, and kisses my knuckles. "Thank you, fair lady, for assisting me in my quest to find Camelot."

"This is a parking lot, not King Arthur's kingdom."

"But you have saved me." He kisses my hand again, then winks. "I'll repay that debt any way you want, Dr. Griffin."

"Uh, sure, whatever." I pull my hand out of his grasp. "See you on Monday at eight o'clock."

"For a clandestine liaison in your office?"

"No, for the first day of classes. Business analytics starts at eight. Please be on time."

His lips slide into a smile that's too damn sexy for my sanity. "How will you punish me if I'm late?"

"Goodbye, Mr. Hunter."

I hustle toward the cafeteria and pray Nick doesn't follow me there.

That man will drive me insane—and I can't swear I won't love every minute of it.

Chapter Three

Nick

I think Dr. Griffin assumed I was lying when I said I forgot where I parked my car. But I told the truth. Honestly, I did. Yes, all right, I waylaid her on purpose so I could talk and flirt with her, but losing my hired car was no ploy to stay close to her. That was an unexpected benefit of forgetting which bloody lot I'd parked in. This campus is larger than I remember these places being back in the Dark Ages when I'd last attended university.

Dr. Griffin wants me. I can tell that much. But she's so bloody determined to deny her attraction to me. That only makes me want her more. One way or another, I will convince her to tell me her first name. I have to. Calling her Dr. Griffin will get old fast.

Now that I've found my car, I drive back to my flat. Rick chose it for me, so naturally, it's the size of Buckingham Palace, though it doesn't come with butlers or any sort of lackeys who might bow down before me. Not sure I'd like having lackeys, anyway. And all right, I admit the flat isn't quite as big as Buckingham Palace. I exaggerated for effect, though it is too big for one bloke who hasn't gotten a leg over with a bird in months and probably won't anytime soon.

Bloody hell.

I arrive at my temporary home feeling hungry for more than food. Yes, I'm thinking about my sexy adviser and all the ways I'd love to help her loosen up. Maybe I'll even offer her a "special" massage.

No, you ruddy moron, you won't do that.

Since I've already been painted as a gigolo, why shouldn't I act like one?

Because I'm trying to save my business, that's why. My employees back home are counting on me for their livelihoods. I have to behave like a mature adult. Most of the time. Even a businessman gets time off for good behavior, though I prefer my time off to involve bad behavior.

With Dr. Griffin.

I take the elevator up to my third-floor flat and unlock the door with my keycard. Yes, my brother set me up with a flat that has high-tech security, not boring old keys you have to stick into the slot and turn. How can anyone be bothered with that these days? Once I'm inside, I kick off my boots and drop onto the couch, propping my feet on the coffee table.

Then I ring my brother.

"What trouble have you gotten yourself into now?" Richard asks the second he picks up the call, without even saying hello first.

"Trouble? Me?" I make a derisive noise. "I'm a perfect angel."

"A fallen angel, maybe." Rick's tone turns serious. "How are you, Nick? Did our plan work?"

"Do you mean the plan where I flee the country and hide out in the desert, far from everyone and everything I know? Yes, it worked brilliantly."

"Are you homesick?"

"No. I'm…adjusting. That's the best I can do."

He sighs. "I'm sorry. Wish I could do more to help you out of this mess."

"Why are you apologizing? You didn't start the rumor that ruined my life." I take a deep breath and let it out slowly, to calm my nerves. "Those lawyer mates of ours are working on it. I'm sure things will settle down soon, and Lady Prescott will find another way to amuse herself."

I have no idea what "it" is, but I do know Chance Dixon and Rory MacTaggart have joined forces to search for a legal remedy to my problem. Would suing the so-called lady who slandered me help at all? Probably not.

Rick and I talk for a few more minutes, but it's seven hours later over there. We say goodbye so my brother can crawl into bed with his lovely American fiancée, Maddie Solberg. Richard had been a workaholic until he met her, and Maddie had been work-obsessed too. Now, they both are doing exactly what they want when they want and taking plenty of time off to enjoy their shared life.

Sometimes I envy Rick. He has a perfect life these days.

Of course, he did suffer through a legal battle with a duplicitous author and wound up settling the suit rather than fighting it. I know he's gotten past all that. Maddie played a big part in helping him cope and build the life he wanted, with her. I don't see myself getting married, but it would be nice to… I don't know. Find a bit of what Richard has.

But I don't have a woman like Maddie, so I toss a frozen dinner into the microwave and eat it while watching a bloody awful reality show on the telly. Then I go to bed. At nine o'clock.

In the morning, I get dressed and drive to campus. Today, I've chosen clothes that might impress Dr. Griffin more than my jeans and Arsenal shirt had. Maybe she doesn't like football. She liked me dressed that way—I could see it on her face—but it's obvious she thinks I'm a tosser who doesn't take school or work seriously. This morning, I intend to prove her wrong. What is my ensemble for the day?

A light-grey suit without the tie, a light-blue shirt, and black Oxford shoes.

I hope Dr. Griffin likes my outfit.

Why on earth do I care?

Because I'm impressing the woman I plan to seduce. If I can't get a proper cuppa in this country, I can at least have a proper shag.

This time, I make a note of which lot I parked in and which space. They have numbers on the parking meters, so it isn't too difficult to make sure I won't lose my car today. *What a sodding moron you are.* Yesterday, I was. This morning, dressed like a gentleman who's posh but not uptight, I am ready for action.

Every woman I pass glances at me with appreciation.

I find myself standing up straighter and walking with more confidence. There's nothing like female appreciation to put a spring in a bloke's step.

The door to Dr. Griffin's office is open, so I walk right in.

She's sitting behind her desk, staring at her computer screen. Those reading glasses perch on her nose.

Even that turns me on.

"Good morning, Dr. Griffin," I say as I stroll past her desk and drop into the chair across from her. I prop my feet on the desk's edge, crossing my ankles. "You look gorgeous this morning."

She turns only her eyes, which are large and unblinking, to look at me. "What are you doing here? Classes don't start until Monday."

"But I'm in desperate need of advising."

Dr. Griffin does look incredible today. I got a good look at her outfit when I walked into her office. She's wearing a skirt that molds to her hips and thighs, a blouse that clings to her bosom, and open-toed shoes that have just enough of a heel to make her ankles even more enticing. She's tied her hair back in a loose bun again. The reading glasses she'd worn yesterday, with their half lenses and pink rims, complete her ensemble.

And all of it makes me want to shag her right here on her desk.

"Please don't waste my time, Mr. Hunter," she says, swiveling her chair to face me. "I have lots of work to finish today, and babysitting you isn't on my to-do list."

Babysitting? She's trying to annoy me, for sure.

Suddenly, I have a brilliant idea.

"Maybe I can help you," I say. "With your work, I mean. I have run a business for years, which means I know how to get things done."

Dr. Griffin bites her bottom lip while roving her gaze over my entire body. "Why aren't you wearing cowboy boots anymore?"

To impress you.

I think those words, but I say, "I'm trying to project a professional image. Studying business is a serious endeavor, so I thought I should look the part."

"Undergraduates don't wear suits." Her brows pull together over her lovely nose. "Come to think of it, neither do grad students or faculty."

"But you dress well."

"I'm the exception. Most professors go business casual these days." She twirls a lock of hair around her finger, over and over, probably without realizing she's doing that. Her gaze wanders over me again. "I, um, like your suit. It's very…professional."

"Thank you." *Can I get a leg over with you now?* I keep that question to myself. "Check your email. I've sent you something I thought you'd like to see."

"What is it?"

The look on her face almost seems like fear. Does she think I've sent her a demonic message that will drag her into Hell?

"It's my business plan," I say, "the one I drafted when I opened my day spa. Since you're my adviser, I wanted you to see it."

And yes, for some strange reason, I need her to read my business plan and be impressed. I can't figure out why I care what she thinks of me, but I do. I need this woman to see me as a mature man who takes his work seriously.

"How did you get my email address?" she asks.

"Faculty emails are listed on the university website."

"Oh. Right." Dr. Griffin's eyebrows draw together, but she does start fiddling with her computer, so I assume she's reading the document I sent her. After a moment, her brows lift. She swerves her gaze to me. "You wrote this?"

"That's right. I found a template online and fleshed it out with details relevant to my company."

"It's, um…quite good, actually."

Why does she sound so bloody surprised?

"I'm glad you approve," I say. "Now, let me help you, please. It'll make me feel useful."

"I have a graduate assistant. Don't need another helper."

"Where is the lovely Lana? I hope I didn't scare her off."

Dr. Griffin snorts like she's trying not to laugh. "Scare her? I think every coed on campus is lusting after you."

Her eyes go wide, but only for a second. Then she clears her throat and starts rearranging the papers on her desk.

She's embarrassed. But why? She said the coeds, meaning female students, lust after me. But she must feel the same way, or else she wouldn't be embarrassed by what she told me.

Perfect. I want her to think of me that way.

"I appreciate the offer," she says, still focused on her papers, "but I don't need any more help. Have a good day, Mr. Hunter."

She's dismissing me.

Oh no, I'm not that easy to get rid of.

I leap out of my chair and lean over her desk with my hands planted on it.

Her head jerks up, and she stares at me without blinking.

"What's your first name?" I ask.

"None of your business."

"Come on, we're both adults. And I spoke to a couple of students—men, not coeds—who told me most of the professors here prefer to be more casual. They ask students to use their first names."

She swallows hard enough I can see the movement in her throat. "I don't—That's—"

"I won't tell anyone, and I'll call you Dr. Griffin when other people are around. Your name can be a secret between us."

"Well…" She glances around as if she's expecting to see a crowd of students hovering outside the doorway, listening to our conversation. Then she blows out a breath. "Siobhan."

"That's a beautiful name. Why don't you want anyone to call you that?"

She twists her mouth into an adorably exasperated expression. "If I pronounce my name, people don't know how to spell it. If I write it down for them, they don't know how to pronounce it."

"Don't worry, I can do both. S-I-O-B-H-A-N. That's how it's spelled."

I've always loved that name. It looks complicated to pronounce, but it's actually quite simple. Shi-vawn. What's so bloody hard about that?

"Thank you for trusting me with your name, Siobhan."

"Sure, whatever."

"Now, getting back to those randy coeds…" I lower my voice and slant in even closer. "Tell me, Siobhan, are you lusting for me too?"

Chapter Four

Nick Hunter has leaned in so close I feel his breaths on my lips and smell his aftershave. God, he smells good. His blue eyes hover inches away. He has the most beautiful eyes I've ever seen, but it's the nearness of his lips that makes me heat up from my skin down to my sex. I've never craved a man the way I'm craving him right now. I know it's insane, and I'm probably having some kind of psychotic episode that's triggering my lust for Nick Hunter, but I can't squelch it.

"Well?" he says, his voice soft and sensual. "Are you lusting for me, Siobhan? I'm lusting for you."

No man has ever told me that. They might say they want me or they think I'm hot, but nobody has ever mentioned lust. I can't remember any man ever gazing at me with so much desire either. Nick isn't devouring me with his gaze, and though his interest is unmistakable, it's also somehow…relaxed.

With his breaths reflecting off my lips, I have trouble thinking. Nick is gorgeous and sexy—smart too, based on the part of his business plan I've read. I might've misjudged him. I'm not interested in a relationship, but maybe I could indulge in a one-night stand with this man.

I shouldn't. It's a bad idea, especially since I'll be seeing him four days a week all summer. How can I have a one-nighter with a student? Well, it could be more than one night. A summer fling, maybe?

My mind is still trying to work out how I can screw Nick Hunter without any consequences when my body makes the decision for me. I can't stop myself from molding my mouth to his. The second our lips touch, an electric current rushes through me, raising every hair on my body and stealing my breath away. His lips feel soft and warm, and they taste faintly of…tea? Guess he found Starbucks after all. I lean in closer to kiss him with more pressure, and when he opens for me, I can't stop myself from plunging my tongue between his lips to savor his mouth.

He slips his tongue between my lips too, groaning so softly I almost don't hear it. But the sound cranks up my lust to the highest setting. Why does he taste so good? Feel so good? The way he coils his tongue around mine makes me moan with the deepest satisfaction I've ever experienced. I need more than a kiss. I need Nick Hunter inside me.

An icy blade of panic stabs into me.

I jerk away from him, rolling my chair backward to get more distance from the irresistible man in front of me. "I'm sorry. That was an accident."

"Accident?" He smirks, and he doesn't back away. Nick still has his hands on my desk and his attention riveted to me. "You'll have to explain to me how you accidentally crashed your mouth into mine. Not sure my insurance covers head-on collisions with the sexy lips of a mathematics professor."

"I meant I didn't mean to do that." Okay, yes, I completely did it on purpose, but I wasn't thinking clearly at the time.

Nick straightens, but he keeps smirking.

Damn, that's hot. I've never liked that expression on anyone else, but he does it with so much steam roiling behind it that I can't help loving his smirk. God, he is irresistible. But I *will* resist him. No one-nighter, no summer fling. Nicholas Hunter is my student, period.

"All right," he says, sighing like I've refused to give him that big bowl of candy he'd wanted. "I'll see you on Monday, Dr. Griffin."

With that, he walks out of my office.

Nick is going to drive me insane. I can't blame him, not entirely, because I'm the one who can't control my lust for that man. I've never met anyone like him. Sometimes he acts like a frat boy, but other times, he behaves like a mature businessman. No matter which persona he adopts, he's always hot and lickable. Oh yes, I'd love to rip his clothes off and lick him from head to toe and back again.

My daughter thinks I need to get laid.

Could she be right about that?

I do my damnedest not to think about Nick Hunter for the rest of the day, creating lesson plans with a single-minded focus like none I've ever marshaled before. Okay, maybe formulating those plans is making me go cross-eyed and giving me a headache, but I need the distraction. Otherwise, I will hunt Nick down, kidnap him, and tie him to my bed so I can screw him all weekend.

This is Friday, after all. No work for the next two days. What else am I going to do? TV gets so boring, and I live in an apartment, so I don't have a garden to tend or a lawn to mow. It's either TV, grocery shopping, or…

Nick Hunter.

Yeah, my kidnapping idea sounds better and better every second.

I do have the address of his apartment. It's in his student record.

No, no, no. I will not go there.

As I rush out of the building, heading for my car in the faculty parking lot, I call Felicity to ask if she wants to spend the weekend hanging out with her mom.

"Sorry, I can't," she says. "Got a job at the cafe on campus. I'm working all weekend."

"Oh. Well, I'm glad you're taking the initiative."

But I wish my daughter could be here to distract me from the British lollipop known as Nick Hunter. No, he's more like a caramel candy, the kind that's hard and melts in your mouth.

"Why don't you call the British hottie?" Felicity asks in a sneaky tone. "I'm sure he'd love to curl up with you on the sofa and—"

"No. Nothing like what you're implying will ever happen."

"I was going to say 'watch the Discovery Channel together,' but whatever you were thinking sounds like lots more fun."

"Please, let's never discuss this subject again."

"Just want you to have fun, Mom. Getting a boyfriend wouldn't kill you."

Actually, it might. Men have a habit of ripping me to shreds. "Goodbye, Felicity."

I drive home and make dinner to distract myself. After I've eaten and washed the dishes, I search for another way to keep from thinking about Nick. About his body, his eyes, his lips. They'd felt so good and tasted even better.

So much for TV as a distraction. Reading a magazine doesn't help either. I try crossword puzzles and sudoku, but that also doesn't work. I can't contemplate lesson plans because I finished all of those earlier today. Giving myself a manicure and a pedicure takes all of ten minutes, and vacuuming doesn't eat up enough time either. What else can I do?

Well, I could use a shower. I usually do that in the morning, but I forgot today. Why? Because of *that* man. I'd been so distracted by thoughts of him that I almost forgot to eat breakfast too.

Nick Hunter. His eyes, his body, his mouth, his voice. I'd loved the feel of his tongue sliding over mine and the scent of his aftershave.

I have two options here. One, I race over to his place and ride him like a bucking bull. Or two, I take care of my lust the sensible way. If there's such a thing as being sensible when I'm consumed with lust for that infernal man. Infernally hot, that is.

Okay, I'm going with the pseudo-sensible option.

That means I go in the bathroom, strip off my clothes, and get into the shower with my vibrator in my hand. It's waterproof, naturally. So yes, I've done this before—but never have I needed to do it as much as I do tonight. Strictly to aid my self-administered sexual experience, I let my mind treat me to fantasies of Nick Hunter. What does he look like naked? I imagine him having plenty of muscles and strong thighs. His cock is big and thick, of course, but it fits snugly inside me when he starts thrusting.

I switch the vibrator on and do to myself what I'm imagining him doing to me. The vibrator isn't as big as I imagine, or maybe hope, Nick's cock will be. But it gets the job done. I thrust it in and out, slapping my free hand on the tile wall while I gasp and mumble the name of a certain Brit who's driving me insane with lust. I come so quickly and so hard that I almost fall down. The shout that bursts out of me couldn't have been heard by any of my neighbors. Could it?

But I don't feel much relief from what I just did.

So I finish my shower, getting clean instead of dirty, and hurry to my bedroom to try again to vanquish my lust for Nick Hunter. I do it again and again and again, then I give up on ever curing myself of this hunger.

There's only one way to get rid of it, but I will never have sex with Nick.

Not this weekend, anyway.

Chapter Five

Nick

I arrive on campus at a quarter to eight Monday morning so I won't be late for my first class. That's the one Siobhan is teaching, business analytics. I talked to my mate Grey Dixon on the phone over the weekend, and he gave me some pointers because he knows all about that technical malarkey. It seems like gibberish to me, but I have set myself the goal of learning new things, and this class is a good place to start.

Since my teacher liked my suit the other day, I've put on another one this morning. This suit is dark blue, which I've been told brings out my eyes. The American wives of my mates, who have joined a club started by the American wives of our Scots mates, declared I have "the dreamiest blue eyes on earth." They gave me a certificate that says so.

When I walk into the classroom ten minutes early, only one person is there. It's Siobhan, of course. She's flipping through a stack of papers while standing behind the desk that sits at the front of the room. The desk comes up to her waist height, so all I can see is her upper body. That's enough. My dick jerks when I take in the vision of that sexy woman dressed in a blouse that clings to her figure and accentuates her breasts.

I need to fuck her. Right now.

But I won't do that. Starting my reborn academic career by sexually harassing a professor seems like a bad idea. I've got enough gossip about me making the rounds, and I don't need more trouble.

Siobhan closes her eyes and rolls her neck like she's working out stiffness, then she clasps her hands behind her and leans backward. The movement pushes her breasts up and out.

Maybe I should quit school. That woman's body is going to make me do things I should not be doing, things like hiking up her skirt and taking her on that desk.

I cough into my fist, not entirely to get her attention. "Good morning, Dr. Griffin."

She jumps. "Oh, I didn't see you there. Good morning, Mr. Hunter."

"Is there any chance I could convince you to call me Nick?"

"Probably not."

That wasn't a firm no, was it? Probably not, she said.

"Take a seat," she tells me, gesturing toward the rows of desks. "Class will start soon. Do you have your textbook?"

I hold up the computer bag I've been carrying over my shoulder. "It's on my laptop. The bloke in the bookstore told me almost no one uses physical books anymore."

"That's true." She goes back to flipping through those papers.

And I take a seat in the first row, directly in front of her desk.

Siobhan glances up at me several times, furtively, like she thinks she needs to hide the fact she wants to look at me.

I don't bother to be sneaky about it when I look at her. She can, I'm sure, see my desire for her on my face, but I don't care. Desire isn't a crime. Or maybe it is in America, who knows. I'll ask my mate Chance about that sometime. He's a lawyer, after all. He also lives in this country, in New Hampshire, so I could even go visit him.

Will I have time for that? Summer classes are four days a week. I'll be going home for Rick's wedding in a month, but that's on a weekend, so I won't miss any classes.

A young woman walks into the room, marching straight to Siobhan.

My teacher glances at the girl with surprise. "What are you doing here?"

"Told you, I want to audit one of your classes."

"Business analytics? Do you even know what that is?"

"No. That's why I'm here. Duh. To learn what this class is all about."

This girl is taking the piss out of her teacher. Maybe I've given Siobhan a bit of a hard time, but I'm not an average student. I suppose my age doesn't give me the right to tease my teacher or flirt with her. I'm not as sarcastic as this girl, though.

She has the same amber eyes as Siobhan, though her hair is brown rather than raven. They do sort of resemble each other.

Dr. Griffin gives the girl a look of motherly disapproval. "This is an advanced course, Felicity. You're a freshman."

"Are you kicking me out of your class?" Felicity glances my way and grins when she sees me. "Hey there, who are you?"

"I'm Nick Hunter, the world's oldest undergraduate."

Siobhan puckers her mouth, but it seems like an attempt to quash her amusement rather than annoyance with me.

Felicity wags her eyebrows. "You're the British hottie, aren't you?"

I can honestly say no one has ever called me that before. "I'm British, yes. What gave me away?" I wink. "Must've been my posh clothes."

She laughs. "I'm Felicity Griffin. You must know my mom since you're sitting in her classroom."

"Dr. Griffin is your mother?" I glance at Siobhan, who seems to be rearranging her papers without actually looking at them since her gaze keeps flicking between me and Felicity.

"Yeah," the girl says. "I'll be majoring in math when I start classes in the fall, but I wanted to see Mom in action first."

I pat the chair next to mine. "Why don't you sit beside me, Felicity?"

"No," Siobhan exclaims, her eyes wide. "She's auditing this class, which means she's not enrolled. I, uh, always tell guests to take a seat at the back."

"But I need to make friends here, don't I? And I'm sure your daughter will be as friendly as you are."

Felicity grins again and settles into the chair beside mine. "I've never met a Brit before."

"I've never met a professor's daughter before."

More students begin to trickle in, and soon the seats are filling up. One girl, a redhead who wears tiny shorts and a tube top, pauses at my chair. She slides her gaze up and down my body, her mouth slanting into a sly smile.

"Wow," she says, "we've got a real hottie in our class. I like older guys. Please tell me you're not Dr. Griffin's boyfriend, then maybe we can hook up later."

"I appreciate the offer, but I'm, ah, busy. And I'm a student, not Dr. Griffin's boyfriend."

The girl flutters her lashes at me. "Love your accent. If I'd known business analytics came with a British stud, I would've signed up for this class when I was a freshman."

"Sit down, please," Siobhan says in a stern voice. "Class is about to begin."

I think she might be jealous of the girls who keep staring at me and speaking to me. Is it my fault women like me?

Dr. Griffin begins her lecture by explaining to us the rules of the class and giving us a preview of the topics we'll learn about. She relaxes the longer she talks and even makes a few jokes. Though Felicity is sitting right next to me, we don't speak once her mother starts the lecture. I take notes on my computer, and Felicity keeps glancing at what I've typed, then nodding as if she approves. I'm not sure the approval of a freshman means much, but I decide it's her way of being friendly when we can't speak to each other.

Siobhan is a wonderful teacher. I've never enjoyed learning as much as I do today, listening to her explain about numbers in a way that makes math sound exciting.

When the hour is up, students file out of the classroom.

Felicity waits until everyone else has left, then she stands and smiles at me. "Maybe we'll hang out again sometime. I mean, you could start dating my mom and then—"

"I'd better stick with being a student only. Wouldn't want to violate the ethics code."

She snorts and waves a hand to dismiss my statement. "You're way too old to worry about that. The ethics code is for, like, pervy profs who try to mack on undergrads."

I have no idea what she just said.

"Felicity," Siobhan says sharply. "Leave Mr. Hunter alone."

"Sure thing, Mom." Felicity heads for the door but pauses on the threshold to throw her mother a sassy glance. "I like him. Better snap him up before somebody else does."

Felicity leaves before her mother can respond.

I get up, stretch, and amble over to my teacher. "Alone at last. If you want to snap me up, I'm game."

"Do you ever stop flirting?"

"Yes. When I'm asleep."

"I see." She collects her papers and stuffs them into an attaché case. "Are you going to wear a suit every day? Students don't dress that way."

"But I'm not a normal student." I lean my hip against the corner of the desk. "You've already kissed me once. Doesn't that break your precious ethics code? Might as well keep violating it in every way imaginable."

"I could get fired for sleeping with a student."

"Did I mention sex?" I tip my head to the side, studying her. "Maybe you're the one who can't stop making passes at *me*. Not that I mind. I love it when a woman wants to seduce me."

"I am not seducing you."

Since her cheeks have turned slightly pink, I think she might be lying.

"What do you call that kiss?" I ask. "Felt like you wanted to undress me right there in your office."

"Anything I might have been thinking about at the time is none of your business."

"Have it your way." I retrieve my computer bag, and as I pass by her desk again, I say, "If you change your mind, just ring me. I'm always available for you."

"But I'm always unavailable for you."

"I love a challenge." I lay a hand on the desk, slanting in. "By the way, I enjoyed your class. You're the best teacher I've ever seen."

Her eyes widen, but she doesn't speak or move.

I walk toward the door.

She races after me, her heels ticking on the floor, and seizes my arm to stop me.

"Did you want to say something else?" I ask, turning toward her.

"No. I, um…" She glances around like she's making sure no one else can hear our conversation. "I shouldn't have kissed you, but I don't regret it."

"Not worried about ethics anymore?"

"I should be, but no." She moves closer, her body inches from mine. "I want to do that again."

"You are a very confusing woman, Siobhan."

"Sorry. I don't mean to be, but I've never been so attracted to a man that I can't think about anything else." She fingers my lapel, her gaze focused on the movements. "You look so good in a suit. This one is even sexier than the suit you wore on Friday."

"I'm glad you like my clothes." Though I'd rather be naked with her.

"This is a bad idea, I know that. Can't help it, though."

"Having a conversation is a bad idea?"

She shakes her head. "Kissing you again is a bad idea."

"The worst ideas are often the most fun."

"Yeah, they are." She lifts her gaze to mine. "Kiss me, Nick."

For a moment, I just stare at her. The uptight professor who told me she would never violate the university's code of ethics has asked me to kiss her. Sure, I've wanted her since the moment we met. But I wasn't expecting this.

"Are you sure you want this?" I ask, and I can't believe I'm asking it.

"Yes. Kiss me, please."

I remember the other day when she kissed me, but that had been a simple kiss. Her lips on mine, nothing else. She'd surprised me then, but today, Siobhan has shocked me. I never thought any woman could do that.

What else can I do?

I slide an arm around her waist and pull her close. The breasts I've been fantasizing about for days are crushed against my chest. The warmth of her supple body covers me, and the scent of her fills my senses. God, she smells good. Feels good. Looks good. I love everything about her body, and I have no reason not to do what she asked.

So I push my other hand into her hair, tip her head back, and kiss her.

I felt her lips once before, but this time is different. Her body is plastered to mine, and I can't resist shifting my hand down to her arse even while I cradle her head in the perfect position for a deep kiss. I push my tongue between her lips and groan because she tastes so fucking good. Siobhan glides her tongue over mine, around it, like she's exploring me with every swipe. I go even deeper, devouring this woman as if I haven't kissed anyone in years, though it's only been a few months. Tasting Siobhan feels nothing like anything I've experienced before, and I never want to stop.

But I have to, eventually.

Not yet, though.

She wraps her arms around me, pressing that luscious body against me even more firmly. I want her naked. I want her wet and hot and writhing beneath me. If I backed her up to the desk, I could hike up her skirt and...

I peel my lips away from hers. With our faces millimeters apart, I gaze into her hypnotic amber eyes. "Siobhan, I want—"

She pushes away from me, smoothing her clothes with both hands. "Thank you for the kiss, Mr. Hunter."

"A thank-you? That's all I get? Come on, have dinner with me."

"I can't."

She grabs her things off the desk and marches out the door.

Chapter Six

Siobhan

I begged Nick Hunter to kiss me. For heaven's sake, what is wrong with me? Getting involved with him is a horrible idea. The other day, I had considered the option of having a fling with him, but I later realized that's a horrible idea too. I'll get addicted to him. I mean, that kiss…

No sex with Nick. It would only lead to disaster, and I've suffered through enough of those.

Maybe I could control my libido if he didn't keep wearing suits. God, he looks so good in those. Of course, I'd been attracted to him on day one when he wore jeans and a T-shirt with cowboy boots. I have a feeling it won't matter how he dresses. I'll be lusting for him if he wears a tutu, that's how hot Nick Hunter is.

How am I going to survive an entire summer with him? Seeing the man four days a week?

I get through the rest of my classes for the morning, which is all I have scheduled today, and eat lunch in my office. After that, I hide out in the library to do my work. Immediately after that, I rush home so Nick can't find me again and seduce me into doing things I should not be doing. I want to do anything and everything with that man, but I won't.

Self-control is torture.

Not that I've shown much of that when I'm around Nick.

At home, I get out a box of leftover Chinese takeout. I'm about to pop it in the microwave when my cell phone rings. The second I answer, barely getting a chance to say hello, a familiar voice sends a hot shiver down my spine.

"Good evening, Siobhan," Nick Hunter says. "What are you wearing? Sorry. I meant what are you doing?"

That doesn't sound any less like a come-on, not when *he* says those words.

"I'm eating dinner, alone," I say. "How did you get my number?"

"You're listed in the campus phone directory."

Oh crap. I had listed my cell number along with my office number as a means of making myself more available to students. I've been accused of being standoffish. No one has ever called my cell until tonight.

"What do you want?" I ask.

"Don't sound so suspicious. I want to cook for you. Come to my flat, please."

No, that's not suspicious at all. I'm sure he has no plans to seduce me once he lures me to his bachelor pad.

"You won't violate the ethics code," he says, "if no one sees us together. Besides, it's dinner, not a night of debauchery."

"Sure, I believe that. You have no plans to seduce me."

"I never said that, but I'll only do it if you beg me to."

Maybe I could get a handle on my libido if he'd stop talking in that soft, sexy rumble. And if he could stop speaking with a British accent, that would be great.

"Nick, I don't think that's a good idea."

"I told you, bad ideas can be the most fun." He sighs. "All right. I vow on my grandmother's grave that I will not seduce you tonight. It's a meal, nothing more. I'd like to get to know you. Unless conversation violates the ethics code."

No, I don't think it does. Except we'll be having dinner in his apartment. Maybe that's unethical, I don't know. He's confusing me. I can't think when I hear Nick Hunter's voice in my ear.

"I'm sorry, Nick, the answer is no. I'll see you in class tomorrow. Goodbye."

Though I end the call, I just stand here holding the phone in my palm and staring at it as if Nick might magically step out of it.

I can still hear his voice in my ear, and it's making me tingle in the naughtiest ways.

Maybe that explains why I grab my purse and race out to my car. I exceed the speed limit on my way to Nick's apartment, but I don't care. For reasons I can't understand, I need to see him right now. Once I get to the swanky apartment complex, I take the elevator to the third floor and sprint down the hall until I find his unit.

I hesitate with my finger hovering millimeters from the doorbell button.

This is insane. Completely nuts. But I don't care anymore.

I ring the bell.

The door swings open seconds later, and Nick hits me with a smile that smolders with enough heat to make me instantly wet.

"Siobhan," he says, "I thought you weren't interested in dinner with me."

"I'm not." I take a fortifying breath and dive straight into the deep end. "I want to have sex with you, Nick."

His face goes blank. For several seconds, he doesn't move or speak, though his gaze stays fixated on mine. Then he smiles in that smoldering way again. "You surprise me at every turn, Siobhan, but I'm glad you're here. Come inside."

Nick ushers me into his apartment.

It's huge, with a big living room that features an enormous floor-to-ceiling window. I drop my purse on the floor beside the sofa and sit down.

He sits down beside me. "What now? This was your idea, so you should set the pace."

What do I want to do with him first? I've never seduced a man before, so I have no idea how to proceed.

I climb onto his lap, straddling him, which pushes my skirt up above my hips. "Kiss me, Nick, like you did earlier. But make it even hotter this time."

He slings his arms around me and pulls me close.

Our mouths meet, and heat flashes through me. When he dives his tongue between my lips, I moan and clutch at his shirt. We consume each other with our tongues tangling and our breaths blustering over our skin while I sink deeper into his lap and he moves his hands down to cup my ass. His fingers massage my flesh.

God, I need him inside me. Right now.

I tear my mouth away from his, though I'm still gripping his shirt.

He arches one brow and slides a finger inside my panties, between my ass cheeks.

I'm breathing hard, on fire, and I can't hold back anymore. So I rip his shirt open.

Buttons go flying, clicking as they land on the table behind me and the one at the end of the sofa.

Now that I've shed all semblance of self-control, I lay my palms on his bare chest and rub them up and down, loving the feel of the hairs that dust his chest and the muscles that carve lines across it. I dip my head to lick a swirling path over his chest, flicking my tongue over one nipple and then the other.

He sucks in a breath. "Christ, Siobhan."

I raise my head. "Rip my shirt off. Please. Hurry."

"Are you sure you want me to do that?"

"Yes, dammit."

He grabs my shirt and tears it open. More buttons go flying, clicking down somewhere in the vicinity of his buttons.

I unhook my front-close bra.

"Fuck," he mutters. "Siobhan, you are gorgeous."

"So are you, Nick." I wrap myself around him, tunneling my fingers into his hair and rubbing my breasts on his chest. "I need you inside me, right now."

He opens his mouth like he wants to speak, but I don't give him the chance. I cover his mouth with mine, pushing my tongue deep and moaning at the sensations evoked by the contact. His tongue is hot and wet, velvety and agile, but the roof of his mouth feels smooth. I love the way his cock is getting firmer every second, pressing into me more and more. Never before have I wanted a man like this, with such intense lust that I don't give a damn if I'm making a fool of myself. Nick Hunter knows how to kiss, and he does it better than any man I've ever known.

What will sex be like with him? Phenomenal. I have no doubts about that.

I wrench my mouth away from his, breathing hard, almost gasping. "Bedroom, now, please."

"Are you sure about this?"

"You already asked me that. So can you please shut up and fuck me?"

When I lunge for his mouth again, he holds up a hand between our lips. "I can't believe I'm saying this, but we should stop. Think about it. Make sure you want this."

"For heaven's sake, Nick, I literally ripped your clothes off." Well, his shirt, anyway. "Considering how hard you flirt with me, I thought you'd be raring to go."

"I am, but…" He scrubs a hand over his mouth. "I'm not a bastard, Siobhan. And you've been determined never to have sex with me. Let's take a minute to calm down."

Maybe I am breathing so hard I might hyperventilate any second, but the last thing I want to do is slow down and think. Letting go feels too good.

Nick grasps my upper arms and holds me an arm's length from him, though I'm still straddling his lap. "I like you, Siobhan. As a person, not a sex object. Well, I like your body too. But I…" He veers his gaze away from mine, sighs, and looks at me again. "I don't want to rush things with you."

"Why not?"

"I want us to get to know each other."

Chapter Seven

Nick

Did I just tell her we shouldn't have sex? I've never done that before. If a woman wants me, I'm up for it. Always. Maybe I haven't slept with anyone since that stupid cow set off a firestorm with her rumor about what I do for a living. And maybe I haven't been as up for it as I used to be. But Siobhan Griffin changed that. The second I saw her, I knew I wanted—needed—to have her.

Why, then, am I telling her we shouldn't do that?

I never have sex with a woman without buying her dinner first or cooking for her. Though I'd wanted to make dinner for Siobhan, we never got round to that. She announced she wanted to fuck me, and the next thing I knew, we were on the sofa with her straddling me, and we were devouring each other like we'd both just escaped from prison after twenty years of solitary confinement.

She practically begged me to shag her.

Naturally, I pushed her away and said we should get to know each other first.

Bloody hell. What's happened to me?

I'm not a complete arse, but I also don't stop in the middle of foreplay to suggest we become mates before we get a leg over. I know almost nothing about Siobhan except that she has an adult daughter and she's a brilliant teacher. She knows a lot more about me thanks to my student record and the internet. Did that rumor convince her I'm a gigolo? Maybe she planned to stuff a handful of twenty-pound notes into my palm as she walked out the door after we had sex.

No, I can't imagine she's that sort of woman.

"Get to know each other?" she says with more confusion than seems necessary.

Is it so hard to believe I'd want that?

"Yes," I say, though I probably sound a touch frustrated. Can anyone blame me? "I'm trying to be a gentleman. If you're wanting me to be the sort who shags a bird and never calls her again, I can't do that. I never do that. Maybe I don't believe in waiting for marriage, or even waiting to find out a girl's last name, but I do not fuck someone and then run out the door."

Siobhan stops blinking, her gaze riveted to mine. She bites her upper lip and tips her head to the side. "You mean that, don't you?"

I blow out a breath and sag against the sofa. "Yes, I mean it."

"Wow, Nick, I'm sorry. I—You seemed like—God, I'm such a jerk."

"No, you're not." I set my hands on her hips. "I understand why you might've thought the worst of me. It's that ruddy rumor, isn't it? A nasty woman got angry when I refused to shag her for money, and now I have to defend myself to the world. I am *not* a gigolo."

"I never actually thought you were. But I guess I assumed you'd want to have sex anytime, anywhere, no questions asked."

Am I meant to deny the truth? No, I won't do that. And I can't help smirking when I say, "I am up for it anytime, anywhere. But I don't want you to rush into this and regret it later."

She takes my face in her hands and touches her lips to mine. "Thank you for being a gentleman."

"Once we're shagging, I might not be so chivalrous."

"I love that you know what the word chivalrous means." She clasps her hands behind my neck. "Since you want us to get to know each other, there's something I've been wondering about."

"Ask away."

"That woman started a rumor about you being a gigolo, but I thought prostitution was legal in the UK. Even if you were a prostitute, that shouldn't be scandalous. Should it?"

"The act of prostitution is legal. It's still against the law to be a pimp or a brothel-keeper. And besides, not everyone is accepting of prostitution despite the fact it's not a crime."

"So, did that woman claim you're a pimp?"

I let my head fall back against the sofa, staring at the ceiling. "She wasn't that specific. But since I own a day spa, people started to assume that if I'm offering 'special' massages, my employees must do the same thing. Every so often, you'll see a story in a newspaper about some bloke, usually a politician or a wealthy businessman, who got arrested while patronizing a massage parlor that turned out to be a brothel."

"That's why the rumor spread. Because people think you run a brothel disguised as a day spa."

"Yes."

"I'm sorry that happened to you." She rests her forehead on mine. "I do want to get to know you, Nick. But I really, really want to have sex with you first. Not because of that stupid rumor. Because I like you and I want you. Okay?"

My dick definitely approves of that statement. It twitched when she spoke those words.

"You want to save the heart-to-heart for after?" I say.

"Please, yes, let's get it on first."

I wrap my arms around her and stand up. She locks her legs around me. When I take one step, something crunches under my shoe. Lifting my foot, I see it's a button from my shirt. Or maybe from her shirt. I've never literally torn a woman's clothes off before, but I have to admit I loved doing that, and I loved it when she ripped my shirt open too.

Once we get into the bedroom, I lay her down on the bed. Well, I try to. She keeps her legs latched around me and won't let go even when we both fall onto the mattress.

"You will need to let go of me," I say. "You still have your skirt on."

It's hiked up around her waist, but there's also the issue of her knickers.

She drops her legs. "Rip the rest of my clothes off, Nick, please."

"Ah…how are you going to get home when your clothes are torn to shreds?"

"Can't I stay the night?"

"Sure, but you'll still need clothing in the morning."

Her sexy little smile makes my cock twitch again. She nudges my thigh with her big toe. "I could borrow yours."

I give her slender body a deliberate once-over. "My clothes will fall off you, Siobhan. Not that I mind, but I believe public nudity is illegal in this country."

"Would you shut up and do me already? Sheesh. I had no idea you'd be so talky during foreplay."

"This isn't foreplay. You'll know when I've gotten to that."

I get rid of my shirt and wrestle with my trousers until I've disposed of them too. Never before have I tried to undress while kneeling on a bed, but I don't want to stand up to do it. Not with Siobhan's lovely tits on display and her body writhing in a way that makes my dick throb. Once I'm naked, I yank her skirt down over her hips and get rid of that too.

She removes her blouse and bra and tosses them away.

That leaves only her knickers. They're lace and almost transparent, not to mention so tiny they barely qualify as undergarments. I rip them off, tearing several holes in the fabric, and hold them up.

"Fuck me," I half growl, half groan. "Did you wear these knickers just for me? If not, then you have a bigger naughty streak than I thought. I love that about you, by the way."

She pushes up on her elbows. "Honestly, Nick, shut up."

I toss her knickers onto the floor. "Not the sort of girl who likes dirty talk? I can work with that."

"Wouldn't know. No one has ever talked dirty to me." She gives me a sly smile. "And you haven't done it either. Saying you love my naughty streak isn't dirty."

"I was just getting started." I crawl up the bed on my hands and knees until I'm positioned above her body. "But I'll skip the talking this time. Mind grabbing a condom out of that drawer?"

She reaches into the drawer on the bedside table and hands me a condom packet.

And I get the thing on faster than I ever have before. This woman has made me so randy I can't think straight.

But I refuse to rush this.

I kiss her, slowly, then I crawl back down her body to kneel between her legs. From this position, I have a perfect view of her entire body. "Siobhan, you are the most beautiful woman I've ever seen."

"Thank you, Nick, but for heaven's sake, would you get to work and stop yammering?"

I can't help laughing. "Yes, love, I'll shut up now—and get to work."

She spreads her legs and bites her bottom lip.

Lying between her sexy thighs, I nuzzle her mound and breathe in the scent of her. Though I want to describe to her how good she smells and all the things I want to do to her, I promised to shut up. So instead, I push my mouth between her folds and glide my tongue up and down her flesh until she moans and clutches the sheets.

"Hurry up," she says.

"I can't hurry up making you come."

"Forget that. Skip to the main event." She spreads her legs wider, planting her feet on the mattress. "Fuck me, Nick."

Christ, no woman has ever wanted me so desperately before. I doubt it's because I'm irresistible. More likely, she hasn't been shagged in so long she can't stand to wait another second.

I lift one of her legs and hook it over my shoulder, leaning forward until my face is above hers. Then I open my mouth and say—

"No talking, Nick."

Well, *she* said that.

I plunge into her.

She clutches my arms, and her breaths become gasps that burst out of her in time with my thrusts. I lean into it more, bending her leg more, and drive into her harder and deeper with every stroke while her tits bounce. She makes indescribable noises, like grunts and gasps and moans combined into one sound of intense pleasure, over and over, her eyes squeezed shut.

"Faster," she says, her voice strained.

What else can I do? I take her faster and even harder until the bed starts to thump and creak, and sweat rolls down my temples. Beads of perspiration roll down her skin too, and her mouth is open like she wants to scream but can't marshal the breath to do it. She feels incredible, so slick and warm, her body wrapped around my cock while I fight to catch my breath. I couldn't stop if I wanted to, locked in an almost frantic rhythm with the wet slapping of flesh as the metronome.

Her entire body stiffens, frozen in the moment before climax.

Gasping for breath, I reach down to rub her clitoris.

Siobhan screams while her body grips me.

I can't resist the siren call of her body, of the waves of her climax pulsating around me. I throw my head back and punch into her one last time, my shout choked off by the intensity of the powerful shocks that rack my body and pulse through my cock.

While I collapse onto her, Siobhan's orgasm keeps going, dwindling little by little. Her chest heaves under me, and I'm still gasping. My body has wound up half on top of her with my head between her breasts.

Sweat slicks our bodies.

Bloody hell, I've never come like that before. Apparently, I love it when an uptight woman orders me to stop talking and fuck her.

The woman I just shagged like a maniac brushes her fingers through my hair. "Thank you, Nick. I needed that."

"You're welcome. And thank you, Siobhan, because I needed that too."

She wriggles out from under me, sitting up. "See you in class tomorrow."

"What?" I say as I watch, dumbfounded, while she slides off the bed and searches for her clothes. "You can't leave yet. I promised to cook for you, and I never break my word. Besides, you said you wanted to spend the night."

"Can I borrow one of your shirts?" she asks, holding up her ruined blouse.

Oh no, she's not walking out like I'm her gigolo.

I jump off the bed and drag her into my arms, holding her snug against my body. "No, no, no, Siobhan. I'm not letting you run away because you're so uptight you can't let yourself enjoy a cracking shag. I am going to cook you dinner, then have you at least one more time, probably two or three."

"Nick—"

"Don't say my name in that voice, like you're my teacher and I've been a naughty boy." I realize what I've just said and decide I should amend that statement. "Well, I'd love to do that as a sex game, but your tone implies I'm a child." I slide my hands down to grasp her arse. "I am the man who gave you the best orgasm you've had in a long time, maybe ever. Don't deny it. We both know it's true. You gave me the best sex I've had in my entire life, so stop trying to turn this into a quick, casual thing."

"But I—"

"You said you want to get to know me. How will you do that when you're planning to scurry out of my flat?"

She bites her upper lip, her gaze searching mine, then she shuts her eyes and exhales a heavy sigh. "Yeah, I said that. And I do want to get to know you, but I have, um, issues when it comes to men. The hotter the guy, the hotter the mess I wind up in."

"Is that your way of telling me I'm the hottest man you've ever met? Or do you always beg men to make you come like a volcano exploding and then scurry out the door?"

"Please stop saying I 'scurry.' I'm not a mouse." She winces. "Though I kind of act like one sometimes. I run away at the first sign of…something more than sex. I can't handle another hot mess."

I cradle her face in my hands, suddenly aware of how intensely she's afraid of getting hurt. "Maybe I love to flirt, and I'm not shy about letting a woman see how much I want her. But I have never left a woman in a 'hot mess.' Give me a chance before you decide I'm bad news. Stay for dinner, at least."

"All right."

We're both still naked, I suddenly realize. Cooking in the nude has never seemed like a clever idea to me, so I grab a long-sleeve shirt from the closet and toss it to Siobhan, then I pull on a pair of trousers and my Arsenal T-shirt.

I slap her arse. "Time to eat, Dr. Griffin. I'm starved—for food this time."

Chapter Eight

Siobhan

What is that logo on your shirt?" I ask Nick while I watch him whipping up something in a skillet. He wouldn't tell me what he's making for dinner. When I asked, he hit me with that steamy smile he's so good at and told me to be patient. "I remember you wore that shirt the first time we met, but I still have no idea what that symbol means."

"It's the Arsenal logo. That's my favorite football team."

"Football? I watch enough British TV series to know you guys think football is soccer."

"We don't think it, love, we know it."

"Uh-huh."

"The British Empire existed long before the colonies became a country, so don't look down your nose at our national sport."

"I thought cricket was your national sport."

"That depends on who you ask. Everyone I know prefers football." He stirs whatever it is he's cooking, glancing away for a moment before he aims his baby blues at me again. "My mate Dane Dixon loves bowls, but that's the most boring game on earth. I don't think anyone would call that the British national sport, except for Dane."

He's smirking.

Damn, I love it when he smirks.

I loved it even more when he had his body wrapped around me and his cock inside me, thrusting so hard and fast I felt like I might rocket up through the ceiling and straight into outer space. I came like that too. Hard, fast, and explosive.

No man has ever made feel as good as Nick does.

But I've fallen for one too many bad boys, and I won't do it again. Since I haven't slept with anyone in way too long, I probably shouldn't worry about the deeper meaning behind one "cracking shag," as Nick called it. It was hot. Now it's over.

Unless I take him up on that offer to screw me several more times.

Since I've already shattered the university's code of ethics, guess I might as well crush it to smithereens. Nobody needs to know I had sex with a student. Besides, he's forty years old, not a vulnerable teenager. I hardly took advantage of Nick, though I did boss him around.

Did he like that? He seemed to, but I can't help wondering if he was being polite.

Sure, because men are so often polite while they're screwing women so hard the entire building shakes.

Not that my apartment building shook. The bed did, for sure.

I fiddle with the napkin beside my plate, staring down at it with more concentration than is strictly necessary. I'm sitting on a stool chair at the bar that separates the living room from the kitchen. Nick had put out place settings while I was in the bathroom. This apartment is gorgeous and so big he could host an entire football team in here and have room leftover.

While I pick up a fork and fiddle with it, I ask, "Did you like it when I was being bossy? During sex, I mean."

He grins at me over his shoulder. "I always love it when you're bossy, whether we're in your office or naked in bed."

"It's okay if you don't like it."

"Do I need to say it again? All right." He leans toward the bar, his gaze nailed to mine. "I love it when you order me to do your bidding. It makes me randy."

"Tell me about your day spa. I read your business plan, but I'd like to hear everything that's not in the official documentation."

"You read my business plan? All of it?"

"Mm-hm. I was impressed, Nick. You're more than a pretty face."

He stands there frozen with a spatula in his hand for several seconds. "You honestly thought my business plan was good?"

"No, I thought it was excellent. A-plus material."

"Thank you, Siobhan." He turns halfway toward the stove, hiding his face while he pokes at whatever he's cooking. "Rick told me it was good, but then, he's my brother. And he's polite. He wouldn't tell me it's rubbish even if it was."

"You think your brother is a liar."

"No, he hates lying. But telling your twin brother his business plan is bollocks would be insensitive."

"Wait. You two are twins?"

"Yes. Richard is the level-headed one, and I'm the bad boy."

They must look the same. Probably sound the same too. I've never met twins before. Though I've only met one of them, I kind of feel like I've met Richard too since they share the same face. Or do they? "So you and your brother are twins. Does that mean you're identical?"

"Yes, we are." He pushes stuff around in the skillet, his attention focused on the task. "Though Rick probably wishes we weren't identical, at least lately. He's been accosted on the street by women who want him to give them a 'special' massage. Maddie, his fiancée, has been very tolerant. But it's my fault he's being harassed."

"No, it's that horrible woman's fault."

He shrugs. "Doesn't matter. I'm ruined, and my downfall is dragging Rick through the mud too, not to mention my parents."

I hadn't realized how bad things had gotten for him. No wonder he fled to America.

"How's the food coming?" I ask. "It smells wonderful. My mouth is watering, and my tummy is starting to grumble."

Nick glances at me over his shoulder. "Are you sure that's hunger for food you're feeling? Maybe I need to shag you again right there on the bar."

"I would love that, but right now, I need food."

He grabs two plates and faces the stove. I hear him scooping food onto the plates, though I can't see what he's doing.

Nick spins around and sets a plate down in front of me with a flourishing gesture. "There you are, my lady. Partake of your feast."

"Thank you, my lord. I shall reward you later for your labors."

Why are we both talking like ye olden days? I don't know, but it's oddly hot.

I glance down at my plate and laugh. "Fish sticks and French fries? Baked beans too, huh? That's your grand meal that took so long to make."

"Yes, and you should be honored. I don't make panfried fish and chips for just anyone." He picks up my knife and fork, holding them up for me to take. "Traditionally, this would all be fried. But that makes such a ruddy mess that I started cooking the lot in a frying pan instead. Rick thought I was insane for trying that, but he's a convert now. I also make the best beans you'll ever taste."

"I saw you open the can. Your beans are store-bought."

"But I heated them up in the pan, so it's homemade. After a fashion." He squints at the food on my plate. "I've never cooked beans that way, so I can't swear they'll be as good as the fish and chips."

"I'm sure it's fine."

He stands there, leaning over the bar, with an expectant look on his face.

Okay, I guess he wants to watch me tasting the meal he made for me.

I cut a piece off one of the fish sticks and slide it into my mouth. While I chew, he watches me. Once I've finished my bite, I eat a French fry—a chip, that is—and then some beans. "Mm, very good. Thank you for making this, Nick."

His expression brightens. "You really liked it? You're not pretending so you won't hurt my feelings?"

"No, I like it. Mm, yummy."

"I had to go to three stores to find decent haddock."

"Didn't you buy frozen fish sticks and just heat them in the pan?"

One side of his mouth curls upward. "Yes, but I had a bloody hard time finding frozen fish sticks that didn't look they'd been regurgitated by a rat."

"Yech. Please don't talk that way while I'm eating."

"Sorry." He grabs his plate and joins me at the bar, sitting on the stool beside mine. "Tell me something about you, Siobhan. I know you have a charming daughter. Where's her father? It's not my business, I know, but I can't help being curious."

"Josh isn't in the picture, never has been." Why am I telling Nick this? Oddly, I feel like I need to tell him, and sharing that one tidbit of information has made me feel lighter somehow. "He left before I found out I was pregnant. I was working on my master's degree at the time, and Josh was a grad student too. I fell head over heels for him, but after we had sex, he announced he was leaving to study abroad. I never saw or heard from him again."

"Are you saying the bloke shagged you once and ran away?"

"Yep. I wasn't a virgin when I slept with him, but I was still kind of innocent. I didn't understand how callous men can be." I consume an entire fish stick in about five seconds, but pigging out doesn't make it any easier to reflect on those days. "Josh taught me that lesson. My parents helped out with raising Felicity so I could get my master's and my PhD. Mom and Dad retired to Florida five years ago. I'd been born and raised in Indiana, but I moved to New Mexico once I finished my doctorate. I was offered a position here as an assistant professor. Now I'm a full professor and tenured."

"That's impressive, Siobhan. You did all that while being a single mother."

"My parents helped. I can't take all the credit."

"Felicity is lovely. You should be proud of her."

"I am. She's my greatest accomplishment." I shove two fries in my mouth and chew them faster than I probably should. "I made sure to spend as much time with her as possible while she was growing up. I didn't want to be the invisible mom."

"Sounds like you didn't have much time for dating."

"No, I didn't. Tried dating, off and on, but men always disappoint me."

Nick rotates his stool toward me, eying me with a curious expression. "You think I'll be another 'hot mess' you have to clean up."

"Maybe. I don't know. You're so different from the men I've dated before."

His lips curve into that steamy smile, the one that makes me melt inside. "Well, I did give you the best sex you've ever had."

"True. But maybe we shouldn't do that anymore." I move the food around on my plate absently. "I mean, I'm your teacher and your adviser."

"We've already shagged each other's brains out. Too late to put the genie back in the bottle."

Yeah, he's right about that. Sex with Nick Hunter is…amazing. He makes me feel good even when I'm trying to be annoyed with him for all his flirtation and innuendo. If I'm honest with myself, I love the way he flirts. I love the way he kisses too, and the way he makes me come. Should I give him a shot? See where this goes?

I can't even if I want to. *Ethics code, dummy.*

Nick puts a hand on my thigh. "You're still worried about violating the rules, aren't you? Can't we get some sort of special permission?"

"Not sure. I'll need to think about that."

He sighs. "In the meantime, you want to pretend we're nothing more than a teacher and her student."

Ugh. How can I possibly do that? I remember every second of what we did in the bedroom—and on the sofa—in vivid detail. I'll probably relive it in my dreams tonight too. And tomorrow night. And the night after that.

Could we sneak around? Date incognito? Slink into and out of his apartment to have sex?

Excitement shivers over my skin. Yeah, I like the idea of a clandestine affair way too much. It's not the affair idea, though. It's him. The thought of sneaking around to have secret liaisons with Nick Hunter makes me so tingly and wet that I almost can't stand it.

"No," I tell him, "I can't pretend we've never had sex. But I can't let anyone know we're involved either, not until I figure out if there's a way around the ethics code. You are older than the average student, but I don't know if that will matter."

"Are you suggesting we sneak around like we're having an illicit affair?"

"Yes. That's exactly what I'm suggesting."

He studies me for a moment, his expression impossible to decipher.

I squirm on my stool and poke at the food on my plate. What if he says no? Or what if he says yes? Not sure which is the most likely to end in a big stinking mess.

Nick smiles, and it's even more sizzling than his steamy smile. That expression not only melts me inside, but it heats me up from my skin down to my sex. He slides off his stool and pulls me tight against his body, bending his head to stare straight into my eyes. "Yes, Siobhan, I'll be your secret lover."

Chapter Nine

Nick

In the morning, I wake up with a beautiful woman curled up against my side and her chin on my arm. Siobhan is still sleeping, so I lie here and try not to disturb her. Despite what she seems to think, I am not the sort of arse who sneaks out in the wee hours. Of course, this is my flat, so I can't do that, anyway. But that's beside the point. I wouldn't do it even if I could.

Maybe once we get to know each other, she won't think of me as a playboy anymore. Honestly, I've never been one of those. I love women, but I never abuse their trust.

Siobhan and I wouldn't have enjoyed each other for hours if she hadn't trusted me to keep our liaison a secret. Now I'm her clandestine lover. It's…strange.

I sigh and stare up at the ceiling while I try to figure out what exactly it means to be a woman's secret lover. Will she wear sunglasses, a trench coat, and a wide-brimmed hat when she sneaks into my flat? Or will she insist we meet in a hotel somewhere away from the university?

A week ago, if anyone had suggested I'd wind up in this situation, I would've called them crazy.

Siobhan mumbles wordlessly and wriggles against me.

Christ, she's beautiful. And underneath that straitlaced exterior, she has the heart of a wild woman, at least in bed. I love being the one who cracked her shell and let all that sexual hunger spill out.

Now I'm picturing an egg yolk oozing out. That might be the most disgusting metaphor I've ever thought of. Ah well, Rick is the literary one in the family.

A mobile rings.

I glance at the bedside table where my phone sits alongside Siobhan's. Which one is ringing? I grab the one that has its screen lit up. It says "Felicity" on the caller ID.

The mischievous part of me wants to pick up the call and chat to Siobhan's daughter, but that's not what a secret lover would do. Bollocks.

I nudge Siobhan with my elbow. "Wake up, love."

She moans and wriggles.

"Wake up, Siobhan. Your daughter is ringing you." I tickle her lips. "If you don't answer the call, I will. And you know what sorts of things I might say to your sweet teenage daughter. Hello, Felicity, how lovely to talk to you. What did your mother and I do last night? Well…"

Siobhan springs upright, her eyes wide, and snatches the phone from my hand. Holding it to her ear, she says, "Felicity? Hello?"

I chuckle. "You need to accept the call first. It's still ringing, you know."

"Shit." She swipes to accept the call and starts over. "Felicity? What's wrong?"

The woman I shagged last night, in the most inventive ways I've ever tried, squints at the sunlight coming in through the semi-transparent drapes and plants a hand on my chest for support. "Huh? Well, yeah, I know I didn't come home last night. Sorry. I didn't mean for you to worry."

Ah, the daughter knows, and the mother is panicking. I can tell that by the way Siobhan keeps winding a lock of hair around her finger over and over.

"No," she says in the kind of stern tone I swear only mothers ever use. "You will do nothing of the sort. How do you know where Nick lives, anyway?"

I stifle a chuckle. Felicity must be threatening to come over here and see what her mother got up to last night.

Siobhan scowls at her daughter, who can't see it. "That is not funny. And I wish you would stop joking about casual sex."

Casual? I don't think what we did last night counts as meaningless sex. It was inventive and athletic, yes, but also intimate. I can't describe how exactly, but it was much more than a fantastic shag.

"Goodbye, Felicity," Siobhan says, then she leans over me to set her mobile on the table.

I pull her down on top of me. "What did Felicity say to you about casual sex?"

"She keeps making jokes about it. Telling me I need to get laid, things like that."

"Does she? Well, you should've set her mind at ease and told her you got laid in the best way imaginable last night."

"Do you honestly think I want to tell my daughter that?"

"I was teasing you. Relax, your secret lover knows his place." Not sure I like being shoved into that place right now, but I did agree to this arrangement. I pat her arse. "I'll make breakfast while you have a shower."

"No time. I have a class to get to." She grasps my chin. "And so do you, Mr. Hunter."

"We're alone—and naked in bed. Call me Nick."

"I have to go home and change into clothes that aren't..." She screws up her entire face. "Clothes that aren't an advertisement for what I did last night."

She's starting to regret it, isn't she? I want to argue with her, using hormones and humor to change her mind, but I can tell she's the type who needs to think about what we've done together. I hate doing it, but I know I need to let her skulk out of my flat and scurry home with her tail between her legs.

I'd much rather she have my cock between those sexy thighs, but I won't be getting what I want this morning.

What else can I do? I squeeze her arse. "Go on. Flee from the scene of the crime. I'll have toaster pastries and orange juice on my own."

She jumps off the bed and hunts for her clothes.

Bloody hell. I don't even get a kiss goodbye. Maybe I am a gigolo after all.

Once she's found her skirt and underwear, she grabs the shirt I let her borrow last night. "May I wear this? I'll get it back to you later."

"Go on, wear it all day long. I dare you."

Her lips twitch like she wants to smile but thinks it might be a violation of the ethics code.

Then she rushes back to the bed, bends over, and kisses me. "Thank you, Nick. Last night was amazing."

She puts on my shirt, tying it in a knot at her waist, and walks out the door into the living room. I lie in bed until I hear the front door open and close.

Groaning, I get up and get dressed. Siobhan Griffin is the sexiest woman I've ever met, hands down. But I don't think she realizes what she's done. That woman has turned me into the one thing I've fought for two months to convince the world I'm not.

I've become a gigolo. Might as well give her a "special" massage and have done with it. *That'll be fifty quid, please, cash only.*

No, I will not feel sorry for myself. I agreed to this arrangement, and I won't renege. Somehow, I will convince that bloody-minded woman I'm more than a secret lover.

My mobile rings as I'm parking my hired car in the metered lot on campus. I shut off the engine and answer the call.

"How is it going?" Rick asks. "Have you gotten expelled for seducing coeds yet?"

I grimace. My brother is joking, and he has no idea what I did last night, but his attempt at humor makes me feel…slightly sick.

"No, I've been a good boy," I say. "Don't you have anything better to do than harass me?"

"You're in a mood, aren't you?"

"Did you want something, or is this strictly a harassment call?"

"All right, Nick, calm down. I'm sorry. I had no idea you were so anxious about school."

But it's not school causing me stress. "I have to go, Rick. Class is about to start."

"Are you sure you're all right?"

"Fine, yes, thank you."

My brother finally says goodbye, and I make my way into Rathbone Hall and the classroom where Siobhan is already waiting. A few students have arrived too. I take my seat in the front row.

Siobhan glances at me but immediately swerves her gaze away.

Yes, I'm about to get schooled in more ways than one.

Chapter Ten

Siobhan

How I survive teaching business analytics this morning, I have no idea. Nick is sitting there looking sexy and edible. He tests my willpower even when he's just listening to my lecture. Is he taking notes? I see him typing on his computer, so I think he must be taking down everything I say. Every time our gazes collide, I get warm and tingly all over. My mind tortures me with memories of last night, when Nick had touched, licked, nibbled, and sucked on every part of my body. God, sex with him is incredible.

Stop fantasizing about Nick Hunter.

I'm usually excellent at heeding my mental commands, but today, I can't stop sneaking peeks at Nick. Can't stop remembering last night either. Or this morning. Waking up with Nick had been so…nice.

He finishes typing something on his laptop and looks up at me, his lips curled in the faintest of smiles. He tips his head to the side and skims his gaze over my entire body.

Then he winks.

Why is he looking at me that way? I doubt anyone else saw him wink, but honestly, he's not behaving like a studious, uh, student. He's acting like the man who screwed me for hours last night.

Maybe I'm reading too much into his expression.

I manage to give my lecture without stumbling over my words or forgetting what I just said a millisecond ago. Do I keep my eyes off Nick? Mostly. He is sitting in the front row, and he's the hottest student in the class, so yeah, I can't completely ignore his presence. I think it's one of Newton's laws—any sexy British particle will attract every female particle whether a woman likes it or not.

But I loved being with Nick last night. We created our own little supernova in that bedroom.

The second I announce class is over, everyone except Nick rushes out of the room. He stays seated until every last student has left, then he unfurls his gorgeous body from his chair and saunters over to my desk, leaning against it.

Naturally, he's wearing a suit. The dark-blue one from Friday. And of course, he has the first three buttons of his shirt undone. The man looks like a model, not an overage college student.

I want to throw him down on this desk and rip open his fly.

My inappropriate lust has gotten so much worse. I know what it feels like to have sex with Nick Hunter, and that's not the kind of knowledge a woman can erase from her memory.

But he's just standing there, leaning against the desk, watching me.

"Did you have questions about the lecture?" I ask while I fight the overpowering urge to look at him.

"No, Siobhan, I understood every word you said and took note of it." He pats the laptop case he has slung over one shoulder. "I made notes with this. I believe it's called a computer?"

He says that like he's never spoken the word computer before, but I know he's teasing me. Everything he says and does makes me horny. I need to get a grip. Right now.

So I stuff my papers and pen into my bag and zip it shut. "I'll see you tomorrow, Mr. Hunter."

I start to walk past him, but he lashes an arm around my waist, pulling me close. "You will not treat me like your live sex toy."

Though I should tell him to let go of me, I like feeling his hard body against mine. I like it too much. My body decides that means I want to get wet, which I absolutely do not want to do right now. "Please, Nick, let it go. I can't be seen fraternizing with a student."

"Of course not." He nuzzles my neck. "I love that you're still wearing my shirt."

I've got it tucked inside my waistband now, but yeah, I'm wearing a shirt that smells like him.

Nick lets go of me. "I'll see you tomorrow, Dr. Griffin."

He walks out the door.

Was it my imagination, or did he sound annoyed and slightly wounded when I told him I can't fraternize with him? His expression had stayed neutral, but his voice sounded…different. He agreed to a clandestine affair. How can he be annoyed because I'm sticking to our arrangement?

He said he would see me tomorrow.

I need him tonight. Right now, actually.

But I have more lessons to plan and another class to teach before lunch. Once I finish those tasks, I try to organize my desk. Maybe it doesn't strictly need organizing, but I'll take any excuse to distract myself from thoughts of…that British man. I can't even think his name, which is childish. For heaven's sake, I'm a mature woman who can handle the aftermath of unbelievably hot sex with an inappropriate man.

Nick Hunter doesn't feel inappropriate, though. Being with him makes me wonder if I've been closing myself off for too long. I'd meant it when I told him I want us to get to know each other better. That's dating, not a secret affair. Maybe I can't be seen in public with him, but there are ways around that. I'm getting all sorts of ideas right now.

I swear Nick is telepathic. He walks into my office at the very second I start wondering about the things we can do in public without getting busted for an ethics violation.

Has he unhooked another button on his shirt? That man is trying to drive me insane with lust. All he has to do is walk into the room, and I want to go down on him. In my office. With the door wide open.

"Afraid I'm busy, Nick," I say. "No time for, um, whatever you wanted."

He ambles up to my desk. "What do you think I'm here for?"

"Not sure, but I'm betting it's something that will get me fired."

"Dr. Griffin, you have a filthy mind. I only wanted to give you this." He leans over my desk to hand me…a business card. "Have a good day."

And he walks out the door.

What in the world?

I look at the card he gave me and read the words printed on it. "Nicholas T. Hunter, World's Oldest College Student." Below that, he has listed a URL: www.TooDamnOldForAWebsite.co.uk.

The man is insane. I should not have sex with him ever again.

But he's teasing me, right? I can't figure out why he would go to the trouble of ordering business cards just to make me smile.

I flip the card over, running my finger along its edge. He wrote something on the back too. These words are handwritten. "Anytime, anywhere. Ring me." Nick has excellent penmanship.

But his inscription sounds like a come-on. And I start getting wet all over again.

I pick up my phone and call him.

"Missing me already?" he asks before I can say hello. And of course, he speaks those words in a steamy-hot voice.

"Get your ass back to my office, Mr. Hunter. You haven't finished your assignment."

"Assignment? I like the sound of that."

"Stop talking and get a move on."

He hangs up.

Thirty seconds later—I know this because I've been counting the seconds on my phone's clock—Nick saunters into my office and stops beside my desk.

"You summoned me," he says, "and I must obey my teacher."

"Sit down and shut up."

Nick smirks and drops onto the chair across from me, propping his feet on my desk.

"Feet on the floor," I tell him.

"Yes, Dr. Griffin. Anything you say." He pulls his feet off my desk. "Tell me all about this assignment I need to finish."

"Watch and learn. There will be a pop quiz afterward."

His brows lift. "Will there? What's the subject?"

I push up out of my chair and sashay over to him, gazing down at the man who makes me so hot for him that I want to do things that could get me fired. I bend over so my face is inches from him and my shirt—his shirt, technically—falls open just enough to give him a good look at my breasts. I did stop off at home to change, but I couldn't bring myself to give up his shirt yet. I also exchanged bras, choosing a lacy red one.

Nick fingers the edge of my shirt. "You are a dirty girl, aren't you?"

"How can that surprise you? Or maybe you've got amnesia about last night."

"I remember every minute of it. But I assumed you'd go back to being uptight today."

"Stop making assumptions about me." I kneel between his thighs. "I've got hidden depths you haven't even glimpsed yet."

"Can't wait to plumb them."

He makes a silly metaphor sound so damn hot.

I place one palm on his thigh and unzip his pants with my other hand. His cock has gotten stiffer already. And like last night, he doesn't have any underwear on, so his dick springs free to wave between us. I clasp my hand around it. "You have a gorgeous dick. Smooth and silky, thick enough to make my mouth water, and just long enough to give me shivers when I think about having you inside me again."

"What happened to 'not at work, Nick'?"

"A girl can change her mind."

He leans forward, reaching for my arms like he wants to pull me onto his lap.

"Uh-uh-uh," I say, shoving him backward with a hand on his chest. "Sit back, relax, and prepare to blow your top."

I lick the moisture off his crown and blow a breath across it.

He chokes and splutters.

Oh yeah, I'm going to love making him squirm.

I flash Nick a sexy smile and take him into my mouth.

Chapter Eleven

Nick

Dr. SJ Griffin is going down on me. Am I hallucinating? Or still asleep in bed with her? Maybe none of what's happened so far today is real. Nothing else seems like a plausible explanation for what she seems to be doing to me. This is the woman who said "not at work" and "secret lovers." Maybe she didn't say those exact words. I might have spoken them. But she wouldn't let me spend time with her unless we sneak around, so I'd had no choice. Had I?

Siobhan wraps her tongue around my cock and slides it up to the base of my erection, then she drags it down to the head.

"Fuck, Siobhan," I growl. "Are you trying to give me a heart attack?"

Instead of answering my question, she moans deeply and shuts her eyes. Her mouth glides up and down my skin, and she starts sucking gently.

Christ, if I'd had any blood left in my brain, it's all flooded south now.

A phone rings. I have no idea if it's a mobile or a landline, and I can't think at all, so no chance I'll figure out the answer. I'm breathing so fast my ears have started to ring. Maybe that's what I'm hearing? No, it can't be—

Siobhan massages my balls and sucks harder.

I gasp, grip the chair's arms so tightly it makes my knuckles ache, and grit my teeth. The best kind of pressure bears down on my entire body, settling in my cock.

That phone stops ringing.

Choking back a shout, I push up on the chair's arms without meaning to, and my arse lifts off the seat a little. I feel the climax coming like a runaway train, the need getting stronger and stronger because she sucks harder and pumps faster while making the most erotic grunting noises I've ever heard. My entire body freezes, my lungs too. Shocks fire down my spine straight into my cock, and I couldn't stop this if I wanted to.

I come inside her mouth while she keeps going, and a strangled shout erupts out of me.

Only once I'm done, and she's wiping her mouth with a tissue, do I realize someone might have heard the noise I made. Can't do anything about that now. I'm still struggling to breathe normally, and my heart is still racing like a deranged greyhound. I slump in the chair.

Siobhan tucks my dick back into my trousers and zips me up. She sits there watching while I gradually regain the ability to breathe without gasping and to sit up straight instead of slouching so far down that I might ooze off the chair.

"Christ, Siobhan," I say when I become capable of speech again. "That was incredible. You're bloody brilliant at giving head."

"Never done that before. I looked up instructions online and downloaded an ebook that had even more information."

"You—what?" I gape at her, and I don't feel embarrassed about doing that. "You researched how to give a blow job? And you're serious about never having tried to do this before?"

She nods, biting her lip.

I laugh, though I'm still somewhat breathless. "If you can learn overnight how to give bloody incredible blow jobs, I can't wait to see what happens the next time we have sex."

"You liked it, then?" She seems genuinely surprised by that fact.

Leaning forward, I cradle her face in my hands. "No, Siobhan, I didn't like it. I loved it."

She turns her face into my palm to kiss it. "Time to get back to work. For me, anyway."

"But I haven't repaid the favor you just did for me."

"Later." She stands up and clears her throat. "I'll meet you at your place tonight, eight o'clock."

Someone steps into the doorway behind her.

The man glances from Siobhan to me and back again. "Everything okay in here?"

He's British, like me. Maybe this is the friend she mentioned on the day we met.

My clandestine lover whirls around to face the other bloke. "Sanjay? What are you doing here?"

"A student heard a strange noise coming from in here and told me about it. She thought you might need help."

"No, we're fine. Just talking shop." She gestures toward me. "Sanjay, meet my newest student, Nick Hunter. He's British too. Nick, this is Sanjay Desai, my friend and colleague."

I heave myself out of the chair because jumping up is out of the question right now and approach her colleague, offering him my hand. "Pleasure to meet you."

"Always nice to meet a new student," he says, shaking my hand. "You're not a typical college student, though, are you?"

I suppose that's his polite way of saying I'm too bloody old for this rubbish. He seems younger than Siobhan, though honestly, I have no idea how old she is.

"Yes, I am a mature student," I tell Sanjay. "But Dr. Griffin is helping this decrepit specimen get through the semester. She's my adviser."

"She's an exceptional person. You can't do better than to have her guiding you." He glances at Siobhan. "I'd better get back to my office. Let me know if I can be of any help, Mr. Hunter."

"Call me Nick."

"Only if you call me Sanjay." He nods toward Siobhan and seems to be trying not to smile. "Dr. Griffin doesn't approve of faculty and students using each other's first names. Maybe you can convince her it's not a sign the world is ending."

"I'll do my best."

Sanjay leaves, and Siobhan rests her arse against the edge of her desk, arms crossed.

"What have I done now?" I ask.

"Nothing." She smiles just a touch. "You're much better at so-cializing than I am. Maybe I'm a little jealous."

"I have no idea whether you play well with others, but I'm intimately acquainted with the way you play one on one." I move in front of her, laying my hands on her hips. "You're bloody brilliant, Siobhan. At everything, not just sucking me off like an industrial vacuum. That's a compliment, by the way. Admittedly not the best metaphor, though."

"Let's have dinner together. At a restaurant."

"We can't be seen together in public, remember?"

She fingers the collar of my shirt, her gaze riveted to it. "We can if we go somewhere farther away from campus. Santa Fe is an hour away, and I know several good restaurants there. What do you say?"

"Are you asking me out on a date?"

"Yes." She leans in, splaying her palms on my chest, and speaks in a sexy purr. "Nick Hunter, will you have dinner with me tonight?"

"A tornado couldn't stop me. That means yes, Siobhan, I would love to be your date."

"I'll meet you at your apartment, eight o'clock." She glances over her shoulder at the papers on her desk. "I really do have a class to get to now."

Maybe I shouldn't like that she sounds disappointed, but I do. She'd rather stay with me. I'm positive she would, and for sure I'd rather stay here with her.

If we're dating now, which she says we are, then I feel like I need to know something. "I hope you won't be offended if I ask, but I'm wondering how old you are."

She tries not to laugh but winds up snorting instead. "That's flattering, Nick, but no. I'm forty-two."

"Perfect. I love older women. And younger women. And women my own age."

"You're not picky, are you?"

"No." I kiss her cheek. "See you tonight."

Then I walk out the door.

Women don't often surprise me, but Siobhan keeps doing that again and again. I might've had some...preconceptions about her, and I'd been wrong. She portrays herself as an uptight schoolteacher, but underneath, she's a passionate, inventive, wild, and amazing woman.

And I can't wait for our first date.

Chapter Twelve

Siobhan

Why am I standing in front of the full-length mirror on the back of my bedroom door, studying my outfit like I'm about to meet the President of the United States? I'm having dinner with Nick. It's no big deal. Is it? Sure, we can't let anyone from the university see us together, but this is still just a date. Since we've already had sex, and I went down on him in my office, I don't know if I can still claim this is only a date. It seems like more than that, though I have no idea why.

I love being with Nick, but that means nothing.

One large order of denial to go, please.

My clothes look fine. I don't own anything super sexy, so this will have to do. Not that I care if Nick thinks I'm sexy.

Supersize me on that order, would you? I'm gorging on denial here.

I command myself to stop fussing over my clothes and grab my purse on the way out of my apartment. The drive to Nick's place only takes ten minutes, but it feels like an eternity tonight. I curse at the stoplights that slow my journey and tap my finger on the wheel in rapid-fire movements.

Maybe I'm a little bit excited about our date.

Never have I wished I wasn't a tenured professor, not until Nick Hunter walked into my office and smiled at me. Now, I want to quit my job and move…anywhere with him. Making major life decisions based on the sex appeal of one man is a horrible idea, so I won't be doing that. Not tonight. After three months with him…

I can't promise I won't uproot my whole life for him.

Me? Changing my life to be with a guy? No, I don't do that. Never.

By the time I ring the doorbell of Nick's apartment, I've shed all that nonsense. He's hot, but I am not a lustful coed who bats her eyelashes at every attractive man she meets. I like Nick, I love having sex with him, and I enjoy our conversations too. That's it. I am in full control of my libido.

The door swings open, revealing Nick.

My heart stutters. I swear it does. Warmth shimmers through me, and I suddenly feel a touch breathless.

Dressed in a charcoal suit with a tie and a vest, he looks like Cary Grant, only sexier. Does anyone wear a three-piece suit these days? I don't think I've ever seen a man wearing one before, but damn, it works for him. He's gorgeous. More than that, he carries himself with assurance and grace as he steps across the threshold and shuts the door.

Nick takes my hand and kisses it. "I'm all yours tonight, Siobhan."

Like he wasn't last night? But this evening does feel different, more meaningful, more…something. I can't think straight with him standing there looking good enough to eat.

"Mind if I drive?" he asks. "You've been working hard all day, so you must need a break. I promise to drive on the correct side of the road, meaning the right side."

"I wasn't worried about that." I still can't quite catch my breath, what with his hand holding on to mine. "Sure, you can drive. Should we take my car or yours?"

"Mine is, ah, nicer." He almost winces when he says that. "Sorry. I wasn't insulting your car, but—"

"Relax. I'm not ashamed of my old beater, but I doubt it can compare to whatever luxury vehicle your brother arranged for you."

"It's a BMW 7 Series."

"Oh. Well, we should definitely take your car."

Like a true gentleman from the Hollywood Golden Age, Nick cups my elbow while we walk to the elevator and while we walk out to the parking lot. His rental car is my dream vehicle. I've never seen a BMW in person, and this one is stunning, with its metallic silver finish and sleek profile. The sexy car makes me want to screw my date right now, right here in the parking lot. Nick even opens the passenger door for me and closes it after I get in.

On the day we met, I would never have believed he'd turn out to be like this.

During our hour-long drive to Santa Fe, we talk. He tells me more about his family and especially his twin brother. From the way Nick describes his brother, I get the idea they're not identical in any way other than their physical attributes. Richard is more serious and not likely to do anything impulsive. Nick loves to take risks and live life to the fullest, having lots of sexy fun along the way.

"Rick always had his nose in books when we were boys," Nick tells me. "I was happier chasing girls and playing football with my mates. That's why our father gave his publishing company to Rick and not me."

"But you're smart and capable too. I mean, you own a business."

Nick shrugs one shoulder. "I wasn't the right man to take over Hunter Publishing. We all knew that."

"Did your father ask if you were interested in working there? In any capacity?"

"Well, ah…no. But I understood why he never asked me. I don't have the temperament for it."

"Bullshit." I study his profile as we whiz down the freeway amid the ever-deepening twilight. "You must've been hurt when your father didn't even ask if you wanted a job at his company, much less if you wanted to take over for him."

"I wasn't, Siobhan."

The tightness in his voice and on his face suggests he might be fibbing, to himself if not to me. I'll wait to ask him that question another time when he might feel more comfortable answering.

Why do I care? His family dramas aren't my concern.

I told him this is a date, though. Couples talk about this stuff.

Nick clears his throat. "I've been, ah, wondering about something."

"Go on, ask me."

"You said Felicity's father abandoned you, but I wondered if you've ever been married."

I sink back into my plush leather seat, aiming my gaze at the windshield. "Yeah, once. It only lasted two months. I met Curtis when Felicity was two years old, and I didn't intend to get married, but I fell for him. Curtis was charming and smart, but it turned out he was a liar. He swore he could handle being a stepdad and living with a toddler. But after two months, he'd had enough. Didn't even say goodbye, just left a note for me on the fridge. Snuck out while I was asleep."

"What an arsehole. I'm sorry that happened to you, Siobhan. Can't stand blokes who break their promises."

Yeah, I think Nick would keep every promise he makes. Maybe I've known him for only a few days, but I've seen sides of him that I bet most people never get to see.

I decide to change the subject to something more fun. "So, tell me about these Scottish people you've become friends with. They live in Utah, you said."

"Some of them do. The rest live in the Scottish Highlands, in and around the villages of Ballachulish and Loch Fairbairn. My mate Grey Dixon has a brother who's married to a bonnie Scots lass. Grey and his wife, Jessica, visit them as often as possible. I've been to their home too, but only twice."

"What about the Utah Scots? Do you visit them?"

"No, I haven't yet. But considering how close they are, I might do."

I glance at him sideways. "Maybe I could go with you sometime. To visit the Utah Scots. Are they Mormons or something?"

He chuckles. "No, they're not Mormons. Evan MacTaggart owns a multinational corporation, Evanescent Security Technologies Limited. His wife runs the American subsidiary, Vic's Electronics Superstores LLC. Logan MacTaggart is Evan's cousin, and he's the head of security at Evanescent. Catriona MacTaggart comes to America too sometimes, with her husband, Alex Thorne. He's Grey Dixon's brother, and he owns property in Montana."

"Why does Grey's brother have a different last name?"

"They're half-brothers."

"Oh, I see. Love to hear more about all of those guys and gals, but we're almost to Santa Fe. Better get in the right lane to take the next exit."

"Yes, my queen, I shall execute your every command to the letter."

He smirks and winks at me.

God, I love it when he does that. Nick Hunter makes me feel like I'm the only woman in the world. To him, I suppose I am. Or maybe I hope I am. My track record with men is abysmal, but I'm starting to think Nick Hunter will be different—in every way.

A chill shivers through me, but it's quickly erased by a delicious warmth.

I don't think I'd mind at all if Nick wanted to marry me.

Holy shit, woman, what is wrong with you?

Yeah, it's way too soon to think about a commitment of any kind. But I'd love to find out where this thing between us will lead.

Chapter Thirteen

Nick

Siobhan and I have just sat down at a table in a se-
cluded corner of the restaurant she'd chosen. She's been
here before with friends and colleagues. She also brought
Felicity here for the girl's eighteenth birthday a few months ago,
and Siobhan celebrated her tenure with a private party in this restaurant.

Tonight, we're celebrating our first date.

It feels strange. I've known Siobhan for a matter of days, but I
love spending time with her. She wants to meet my mates—and
my family too, I'm sure—so maybe I should do that. Introduce
her. See how we fare as a couple once it's not a secret. None of my
friends or family would tell anyone about us if we ask them to
keep it quiet. Once the semester is over, we won't need to hide our
relationship.

Will we stay together that long?

Since we're in a U-shaped booth, Siobhan is sitting near me, but
we can still see each other. We chatted to each other for the entire
hour-long drive. I've never talked that much with anyone, not even
my girlfriends. Siobhan, the woman I'd initially dismissed as uptight, has become the best mate I could ever have. I love learning
about her and telling her about me.

Siobhan leans in to whisper in my ear with her lips grazing my skin. "I'm glad we got a booth in the corner where the lighting is smoky and we have some privacy."

"If you're planning to go down on me in the restaurant, I'll be forced to say no. Can't be quiet when you do that to me."

"No blow job, check." She nuzzles my cheek. "But I'd love to make out with you, Nick."

"Let's order first, and make out while we wait for the appetizer."

"Perfect. Let's get champagne too."

"I was thinking the same thing."

A waitress approaches, and we order our meal with appetizers and champagne. We agree to hold off on ordering dessert until after our meal, in case we're too full to eat anything else.

The waitress leaves, and we're alone again.

Now it's my turn to whisper in her ear. "Even if we don't order dessert, I can still gorge on the sweetest treat—your cream."

"If you keep talking that way, I might climb on your lap and unzip your pants."

"We agreed giving me head in the restaurant is a rubbish idea."

"Didn't say I'd give you head. Said I'd mount you and unzip your pants." She lays a hand on my leg, sliding it between my thighs and up until her fingers brush my groin. "I meant I'll fuck you, Nick. Ride you until your eyes roll back in your head."

"You fulfill all my naughty-schoolteacher fantasies."

"Did you really fantasize about that?"

"Every schoolboy does. I think it's in our DNA to lust after sexy women who own rulers and chalkboards."

The waitress arrives with our appetizer, so we go back to behaving like a normal couple who want to enjoy a good meal. While we eat, we keep talking, though not about my schoolboy fantasies. Siobhan tells me stories from her life as a professor and as a single mother, some humorous, others more serious. I love hearing everything about her life.

I hold off on asking her a particular question until we've eaten half our meal. Then, my curiosity gets the better of me. "Before you met me, how long had it been since you had sex?"

She takes a long drink of her water before answering, then she clears her throat and says, "Five years, give or take."

"Five years? But you are a passionate woman."

"I'm also a single mom. After my parents retired to Florida, I didn't have time for dating." She pokes at the ice cubes in her glass, making them bob in the water. "Honestly, I hadn't dated much before that. I slept with guys, that's all."

"Were these one-offs?"

"The sex was, yes, but I had more than one date with each man before we slept together. Eventually, I realized what mattered most to me was spending time with Felicity, not dating. She was growing up, and I knew someday she'd go her own way, without me."

I slip an arm around her shoulders. "Felicity adores you. She wouldn't leave and forget about you."

"You met her once."

"Anyone can see how close you two are."

"Yeah, we are. I'm lucky that way. How close are you with your parents?"

"Not like you and Felicity, but I get on very well with Mum and Dad."

"Good. I like men who love their parents." She leans in, her smile turning slightly mischievous. "Why don't we skip dessert and go home to have sex all night?"

"Are you calling my flat 'home'?"

"It's where you currently live, isn't it? That's the definition of a home." She taps my chest with one finger. "Are you purposely ignoring the fact I just propositioned you?"

"No. But I'm still recovering from the shock."

Siobhan laughs softly. "Oh yeah, I'm sure women never, ever proposition you."

"Maybe they do, on occasion, but I don't have one-night stands."

"You don't?"

"No, I do not. I love women, but using and discarding them isn't the sort of man I want to be."

She clasps my hand. "Oh Nick, you know I've never thought you were that kind of man. I meant that you're gorgeous and sexy, not to mention smart and sweet, so women must flock to you."

"When we first met, you assumed I was a chancer."

"I have no idea what that word means."

"You thought I was the sort who will do anything to get what I want."

She shakes her head, spreading a hand over my cheek. "No, I never thought that. You are the biggest flirt I've ever met, though."

"But you don't think I'm...a gigolo."

"Of course not. I may have read about your scandal online, but I don't believe everything that's on the internet. It's the digital equivalent of neighborhood gossip, only worse because it's widespread."

I slump against the back of the bench and sigh. "I'll need to go home and deal with the consequences sooner or later. But at least you don't think I'm a prostitute or a brothel-keeper."

"Things will settle down. Rumors rarely have long half-lives."

"I'm more concerned with the whole life of this one. Besides, it's been two months, and there's no sign of the rumor dying out."

She wraps her arms around my neck and kisses my cheek. "Let's forget about that for tonight. Take me home and make love to me, Nick."

I can't help smirking. "By 'make love' you mean 'shag like a maniac,' right?"

"Uh-huh. Can you handle that, Mr. Hunter?"

"Oh yes, I can handle you, Dr. Griffin." I push a hand into her hair, pulling her in for a kiss. "And for the record, when I'm with you, I'm always up for it."

Maybe after we've spent more time together, she'll want more than sex that qualifies as an Olympic sport. I want to do more than fuck her. I want to make love to her in the truest sense of the phrase.

I let her take the wheel for the ride home because she wants to drive my hired car almost as desperately as she wants to shag me. How can I resist a lustful, exciting woman? I can't. Whatever Siobhan wants, I'll give it to her.

Unless she wants to throw me over.

I don't like the idea of that at all.

Chapter Fourteen

Siobhan

A few days ago, the thought of seeing Nick Hunter four days a week made me uneasy. Now, I look forward to it. He's not at all the way I assumed he was when we first met. Sure, he's a big-time flirt. And yes, he has a wicked sense of humor. But I love those things about him, more than I ever could've imagined I might. I love spending time with him.

We can't be seen together in public, not in this town. I usually dread the end of a semester because it means I'll have nothing to do for a while. This summer, I'm looking forward to the semester ending so Nick and I can go wherever we want and not worry about someone seeing us.

Every Monday, Tuesday, Wednesday, and Thursday, Nick shows up ten minutes before class starts. He sits at his favorite desk, the one that's six feet from my desk, and he does the most shocking thing.

He pays attention to my lectures. The man genuinely wants to learn about business analytics.

Most of my students pay attention about half the time, distracted by their phones and their personal lives. I've lost count of how often I've needed to confiscate phones and tell students to be quiet.

But Nick never makes a sound unless he's asking a relevant question.

Seeing him behave like a dedicated student makes me so damn hot for him. Every evening, I sneak away to his apartment and beg him to make me scream all night long. He does, every time. But we also talk and laugh and cook together. I haven't enjoyed this kind of relationship with a man...ever.

By the end of week two, we know more about each other's pasts and families than I know about math. I haven't dated much before this, and none of those guys cared about my life. They wanted to prattle on and on about their jobs or sports or some other boring thing. They never wanted to hear about me. Math is too dull.

Nick genuinely thinks it's fascinating.

We're lying in his bed one evening after another round of fantastic sex, when he asks me, "What is pi?"

"It's the ratio of a circle's circumference to its diameter. Didn't you learn that in school?"

"No, I learned pi is three point one four one five nine. And I learned I needed to memorize that so I'd pass my maths test."

"Pi is an irrational number, which means it has no end. It goes on and on without repeating itself."

"Bugger me. Glad I didn't need to memorize all that in school or I'd still be writing my answer."

"Talking about the number pi makes me want actual pie, the banana cream variety."

Nick kisses my shoulder. "There's a bakery down the street. Maybe I could get you some banana cream pie."

"Oh no, you are not leaving this bed until I'm finished with you."

The next evening when I arrive at his apartment, he has a banana cream pie in the fridge.

Nick loves to make me breakfast, often serving it to me in bed, but he waits until a few days later to offer me a particular kind of morning meal. I've just woken up in my favorite way—with Nick kissing my neck and caressing my cheek—when he suggests something different.

"How about a full English breakfast?"

"What's in one of those?"

"More food than five blokes could eat, but you can just sample the offerings." Though he's been seated on the bed's edge, leaning over me, now he straightens and pats my hip. "Your full English will include bacon, bangers, fried tomatoes, beans, and toast."

"Bangers?"

"Sausages."

"Oh. Sounds good, but I should probably avoid beans. Don't want to be flatulent while I'm teaching a class."

"If you insist, though you're ruining my full English."

Sitting up, I throw my arms around his neck and kiss him. "I'll make it up to you later."

"You'd better." He cups my bottom with both hands. "How about pancakes instead of beans?"

"Mm, yum. Dating you will make me gain twenty pounds, but I'll be one very happy woman."

"Don't care if you gain weight." He nibbles on my earlobe. "But I'll give you a good workout tonight."

Oh yes, Nick Hunter always does that. I've developed more stamina since I got involved with him.

He bows his head and clears his throat. "Would it be too strange for me to give you a key to my flat?"

"No, not at all." I didn't even hesitate to say that. Maybe I should feel weird about it since we're keeping our relationship under wraps, but I feel nothing but good.

So Nick gives me a key. No more ringing the doorbell. I'm an official girlfriend now, even if nobody else knows about us.

Every day in class, Nick takes copious notes. I can tell because he keeps typing furiously on his computer. Often, when I arrive at his place after work, I find him poring over those notes. The first time I catch him doing that, I lean over the back of the sofa to see what he's doing, and to skate my palms down his chest.

"You just keep on surprising me," I say, sliding my hands further down until my fingertips bump into the waistband of his slacks. Yeah, he's still wearing his suit without the jacket, the outfit he wore all day. "You've got multi-level lists with bullets and numbers, even highlighted text."

"The highlights are color-coded too."

I grab his laptop and set it on the cushion beside him, then I climb onto his lap—from behind the sofa. "Forget dinner. I need your body, Nick, right now. Your intellectual side gets me so hot."

"What about my businessman side?"

"That's an offshoot of your dedicated-student side."

"I see." He stands up while holding me in his arms. "Your strict teacher side makes me so fucking randy."

"Should we play disobedient student and naughty teacher again?"

"That's my favorite game."

Every new day with Nick makes me happier and more excited for the future—with him.

Do I have a future with Nick? We haven't discussed anything beyond the summer semester, though we both agreed to keep our relationship a secret until he's not my student anymore. Does that mean we'll stay together after that? He lives in England and has a successful business there. Do I want to be with him enough to move to another country for him?

The other day, I mused that I might willingly go anywhere for him.

But I don't get much time to consider the future because I'm too busy with work and Nick.

On a Thursday evening that marks three weeks since Nick breezed into my life with his big feet on my desk, he brings up a subject I don't expect. We're sitting on the sofa in his apartment, curled up together while watching TV.

"My brother's wedding is next Saturday," he says. "Would you, ah, like to go with me?"

"To the wedding?"

"Yes." He squirms and avoids looking at me. "Would you be my date? That means you'll meet my family and my mates."

"Sure, I'd love to go. We'll need to be home Sunday, though, since we both have class on Monday."

"But Monday is July fourth." He smirks. "I understand that's some sort of holiday on this side of the pond, and most people stay home to eat hot dogs and shoot off small explosives. We can come home Monday, can't we?"

"Right. I forgot about that." I push my elbow into his side. "And don't make fun of Independence Day. Like you Brits never shoot off 'small explosives' or glue yourself to your TVs when football matches are on."

"Guilty as charged. I'm an Arsenal fan, after all."

"Which would you rather do? Watch a football game or play dirty teacher with me?"

He scrunches up his face like he's seriously mulling the choices. Then he blows out a melodramatic sigh and squeezes my thigh. "Afraid I'll have to go with Arsenal."

"Oh, I guess you don't want to get lucky tonight, then?"

Nick tickles me until I'm laughing so hard tears are rolling down my cheeks. With me pinned under him, both of us lying lengthwise on the sofa, he suddenly gets a worried look on his face. "Are you sure you want to go home with me?"

"Yes, I'm sure."

"My brother and my parents will be polite, but I can't vouch for the Dixons. Reese can be…well, a lot like me, only younger. Dane and Chance are mature and no bloody fun at all."

He grins and winks, which lets me know he's joking. I would've known that anyway. Nick Hunter wouldn't say nasty things about his friends, or about anyone.

Except for the horrible woman who's trying to ruin his career.

That reminds me of something I've been hesitant to ask. "How's it going back home, with that rumor business?"

"Richard swears it's dying down. We'll find out next weekend if he's lying to make me feel better." Nick kneels between my legs and scratches his head. "If the rumor is still going strong, you might not want to be seen with me."

"Of course I'll be seen with you. I'm not ashamed to be Nick Hunter's girlfriend."

"What about the tossers who have posted memes of me on the internet? I don't want you to get in trouble if someone takes a picture of us and posts it online."

"Don't worry about me. I'll be fine." I get to my knees and hug him. "Let's go in the bedroom and play."

"I never can say no to a student-teacher conference."

Chapter Fifteen

Nick

The next week flies by. Before I know it, Siobhan and I are packing for our trip to England. Felicity can't go with us since she has a summer job and needs to work on the weekend. I'm getting more and more anxious every minute. Why? It's Rick's wedding, not mine. But I don't want to embarrass my brother. What if paparazzi turn up? Sure, because I'm so famous they'll want to slog all the way to Colchester just to snap a few pictures of the village gigolo.

Only locals have bothered to post pictures of me online. No one who isn't from Colchester or Cockshire would know about my scandal. Right?

Siobhan suggested last night that I should "google" myself to find out what exactly is out there concerning me. I was too much of a coward to do it. What if the situation has mushroomed into a national scandal?

Oh yes, I'm so bloody important the Queen herself will chastise me.

This is only nerves. I shouldn't panic.

I'm in the bedroom zipping up my suitcase when I hear Siobhan unlock the front door. No woman has ever had a key to my home, but I couldn't wait to give her one. She's…different. Why else would I ask her to go home with me for Rick's wedding? Maybe I've developed stronger feelings for Siobhan than even I realize. I did buy something special for her two weeks ago, something I want to give her as a surprise if I can work up the courage. That must mean I care about her as more than a lover.

The woman herself walks into my bedroom and smiles. "Ready for the big trip? I'm so excited to meet your family."

"And the Scots contingent will be there too."

"Perfect. My first experience with real live Scottish people."

"You've met dead ones, then?"

"Ha-ha." She glances at my suitcase. "Are you finished with your panic attack yet? I see you've packed, so the trip is still a go."

"Of course it's a go. I'm not that much of a coward."

Maybe I am, though, since I briefly considered barricading the front door to keep her from coming inside and convincing me to behave like a mature adult. I'd thought about hiding under my bed too. Siobhan doesn't need to hear about any of that. Does she? No, I think I can safely keep those things to myself.

But I get itchy all over when I think about keeping the truth from her.

She laughs when I tell her about my barmy thoughts. "Under the bed? You are so adorably weird. And what would you have used to barricade the door?"

"The couch."

Laughter splutters out of her again. "You're the cutest, Nick."

"Are you done mocking my angst?"

"Yes." She fingers the lapels of my suit jacket. "Are you sure you want to dress up for a ten-hour flight?"

I squeeze her arse. "Who says either of us will wear anything during the flight?"

"We won't be alone. That's what you said."

"Right. Evan MacTaggart will pick us up at the Santa Fe airport and take us to England on his private jet."

"It's nice to be friends with a billionaire, huh?"

"You haven't met Evan, so he's not your friend. He's mine, and you are my girlfriend. I suppose that makes him your friend by proxy? Or something like that?"

"Stop racking your brain to sort out that stuff. I need you in top form so I can drag you into the bathroom on the jet and make your eyes roll back in your head."

"We can do better than the loo. Evan's jet has a bedroom."

Her brows shoot up. "Wow, I'm going to love traveling the Scottish way."

"I think it's only Scottish billionaires who travel on private jets. Maybe multimillionaires do too. And a few wealthy Scots who haven't reached millionaire status yet."

Siobhan kisses me and pinches my cheek. "You babble when you're anxious, but it's cute."

Groaning, I rub my eyes. "I haven't been home in a month. Who knows what's happening with that bloody scandal now."

"Your brother and your employees would've told you if anything's wrong."

That's true, but I still can't shake this dread.

Siobhan and I take her car to the airport and climb up the stairs into the Gulfstream jet owned by a Scottish billionaire. The interior is posh and comfortable, but I'm sure I will feel nothing close to comfort during the flight home. I introduce Siobhan to Evan and his wife, Keely. They've brought their infant daughter too. Next, Logan and his wife, Serena, introduce themselves along with Serena's son, Chase. I can tell Siobhan loves meeting them, and she gets commandeered by the American wives of my Scots mates before I can even sit down. The women gather around a small table to chat.

I stretch out on a sofa.

Logan and Evan take the chairs beside the sofa and aim their steady gazes at me.

"Why are you two staring?" I ask. "Did I forget to zip up my fly?"

"No," Logan says with a slight chuckle. "We're under orders from Richard to keep an eye on you. If we notice any signs of mental distress, we're to pour whisky down your throat."

Thank you so much, Rick. You've sicked the Scots mafia on me.

"I don't need whisky," I tell Logan. "But if it's all right with my keepers, I'll have a lie-down."

"Go on," Evan says. "We can watch you sleep and intervene if it looks like you're having a nightmare. Can't we, Logan?"

"Aye, we'll keep an eye on him."

What in the world did my brother tell these blokes? They seem to think

I'm on the verge of a nervous breakdown, but I'm not that bad off.

Logan and Evan find a deck of cards and start a poker game. Though they invite me to join them, I decline. A lie-down appeals to me more than poker since I didn't sleep well last night. I can't sleep now either, though. *Bugger.*

The Scots are enjoying their second game when Siobhan's sweet voice whispers into my ear. "Are you asleep, Nick?"

"No, I'm pretending to sleep. It's as refreshing as the real thing."

"Well, if you can tear yourself away from fake sleep, I have a surprise for you in the bedroom."

I leap off the couch. "Lead the way, love."

Siobhan takes my hand, guiding me between the aisles toward a short hallway. She swings a door open, and we walk into a bedroom that features a large bed.

"I need my own jet," I say. "You and I could live in one like this."

"Are you asking me to move in with you in your imaginary jet?"

"Yes. I'm afraid imaginary is the only sort I can afford."

Siobhan strips off her clothes and crawls across the bed on her hands and knees. "Why aren't you naked yet?"

Why, indeed. I get rid of my clothes as fast as humanly possible. Or maybe I do it faster than that, approaching superhero speed. The chance to make love to Siobhan pumps enough adrenaline through my bloodstream that I'm fairly sure I could carry a double-decker bus on my shoulders.

Yes, we have sex. Three times. And that includes extensive foreplay because Siobhan loves that. We try not to make too much noise since there are two minors on board, including an infant.

I hardly notice when the jet lands.

Siobhan and I emerge from the bedroom just as the pilot is lowering the stairs for our exit. It's the middle of the night here in the UK. We follow our friends down onto the tarmac where my family is waiting. Mum and Dad rush over to greet us, hugging me and then Siobhan—before I've even introduced her.

"Take it easy, Mum," I say. "Let me tell you her name before you maul my girlfriend."

Is this the first time I've called her that out loud? I think it is.

Clasping my girlfriend's hand, I say, "This is Siobhan Griffin. She's a professor at the university where I've been studying."

"Oh, Siobhan," my mother coos, "what a beautiful name for such a beautiful girl. We're so happy Nick you brought you along. I'm Pippa Hunter, and this is my husband, Edward."

My father smiles and nods. "Siobhan, welcome to England. We're chuffed you're here, and I know Rick feels the same way."

Dad flaps his arm until Rick and Maddie approach us.

My brother slaps my arm. "Good to have you home, mate."

"Ah, thank you," I say. Then I tell Siobhan, "This is my brother, Richard, and his fiancée, Maddie Solberg."

"Thanks for telling me that's your brother," Siobhan says. "I wouldn't have known otherwise."

Am I a bloody stupid arse or what? Richard is my twin, so of course she knew who he was the second she saw him.

Maddie laughs. "It's so cute that Nick's nervous about introducing you. The twin thing can be weird at first, but you'll get used to it."

"Can we get going?" I ask. "Siobhan doesn't want to stand on the tarmac chatting to you. We're knackered from the long flight."

Once we arrive at my parents' house, Richard and Maddie say good night and leave, and my mother leads us to my old bedroom.

"I assumed you two would share," Mum says. "But if Siobhan prefers her own bed, she could have Rick's old room."

"No, I'm with Nick," my girlfriend announces.

My mother hugs Siobhan again and kisses her cheek, then smiles at both of us. "Good night, loveys."

I lead Siobhan into the bedroom and shut the door. "Sorry. This was my room when I was a boy."

My girlfriend turns in a circle, her lips curving up more and more as she takes in the decorations on the walls. "Gee, what a surprise. Football posters. Football memorabilia. Oh, and a football itself." She picks up the ball, rolling it between her palms, and gives me a teasing smile. "Of course, Americans know it's a soccer ball."

When I open my mouth to say something sarcastic, I end up yawning instead. "Sorry. I really am knackered. Aren't you?"

"I think I'm so excited to be here that I don't feel tired yet." She drops the football and walks up to me, wrapping her arms around my waist. "But you do look wiped out. Let's cuddle up together in your childhood bed."

"Please don't call it that. Makes me feel like I'm a little boy who's not toilet trained yet."

"Okay. I'll call it Nick's love nest instead." She glances at the bed over her shoulder. "I slept in a twin bed until I went away to college. You had queen size. Hmm, was that to accommodate all your girlfriends? Two or three at a time?"

I slap her arse. "Cheeky woman."

When I yawn, loudly, Siobhan insists we crawl into bed and go to sleep.

Late in the morning, UK time, I wake up with the sweetest and most beautiful woman in the world snuggled against me. I tickle her belly until she opens her eyes, then we have a quick shag before breakfast. Quietly. This is my parents' house, after all.

That afternoon, the wedding festivities begin. Most of my friends are here, including the Dixons and Alex Thorne, plus the MacTaggarts. We all gather in the garden for an informal get-together.

While Siobhan is laughing with the American Wives Club, Alex pulls me aside.

"Are you interested in a test?" he asks, almost whispering. "Like the one Richard had us do for him when he brought Maddie home."

"Rick and Maddie were already in love. Siobhan and I… Well, I don't know how we feel about each other, so I don't think that sort of test is a good idea."

My brother had asked me and Alex to whisper in Maddie's ear to see if she could tell our voices from Rick's. Maddie has a crackbrained theory about all British men sounding similar, but she wasn't fooled by our test. Not even when I whispered in her ear. Since I'm Rick's twin, you'd think I could've fooled Maddie. But no, she was already so in love with my brother that she knew the difference even while her eyes were covered.

Would Siobhan recognize my voice if I covered her eyes? Or would she think I'm Richard? Don't think I'll test her, not just yet.

"Aren't you in love?" Alex asks. "The way you look at Siobhan, I would've said yes."

"Siobhan would not be fooled by hearing your voice."

"Richard is available."

"Thank you for the suggestion, but I don't want to test my girlfriend today."

Alex pats my shoulder and walks away.

Should I ask Richard to… No, absolutely not. Well, maybe… *No, you moron, you will not do that.*

But despite what I told Alex, I find myself marching straight to Richard.

Chapter Sixteen

Siobhan

I have no idea what Nick and his brother are talking about, but they're standing close to each other and clearly whispering. Maybe my boyfriend is plotting something. I did get involved with a sexy Brit who has a naughty sense of humor, so I won't be surprised if those two are up to something, well, naughty.

"You look worried, lovey," Pippa Hunter says. She and I have been enjoying a nice conversation, just the two of us. "Don't worry about Nick and his brother. They like to huddle and plot, though the plotting usually starts with Nick. I'm sure you know what he's like."

"I do, for sure." I drag my attention away from the boys to look at Pippa. "I have to admit, I'm still getting used to the twin thing. Nick told me he had an identical twin brother, but it's different to watch them together."

"Did you know they both developed appendicitis within hours of each other? They went in for surgery at the same time, though with different doctors."

"That's odd. Do things like that happen a lot with twins?"

She laughs. "I've only had the one pair. Can't speak for all the others in the world."

"I hope they can't read each other's minds or feel what the other is feeling." I'm only half-joking. What if they can do that? It would be too weird for words. Not that I believe in telepathy.

"You'll have to ask Nick about that," Pippa says. She glances past my shoulder, then smiles and touches my arm. "We'll chat more later. One of them is heading this way."

"Can't you tell them apart?"

"Of course I can."

Pippa walks away just as Nick arrives.

He hooks an arm around my waist and tugs me close. "I hope Mum wasn't regaling you with stories of my childhood adventures."

"Oh, she told me lots about you. And your brother." I boost myself up on my toes to whisper in his ear. "Do you feel it when Richard has sex with Maddie?"

"No, but I wish I could."

"I'm not enough? You need a telepathic harem?"

"You are more than enough for me. And Rick had better not be telepathically spying on me when you and I are at it."

I drop down onto my soles and slip my arms around his waist."I bet Richard could learn a thing or two from you."

"That's true, but I don't want to share my sexual expertise with anyone, not even my brother."

Snuggling closer to him, I nibble on his bottom lip. "So, what were you twins conspiring about?"

"Rick begged me to give him advice about how to properly shag Maddie, but I told him to bugger off and buy a sex manual."

I know he's joking. Probably. "The wedding is this afternoon, right?"

"Yes. At three o'clock, UK time, which for us would be…" He sighs and shrugs. "Some other bloody time."

"Don't worry. I'm sure your mom will get us there at precisely three o'clock."

"I'm the best man, so I'd better get my arse there on time."

"Are you nervous?"

He twists his mouth into a strange expression, averting his gaze. "That would be bloody stupid, wouldn't it? I'm not the one getting married today."

"Come on, I know you've been anxious about coming home and what might happen with that stupid rumor. Today, you'll be out in public. It's got to be nerve-racking."

"Maybe I am a little nervous. But I don't want anyone else to know, all right?"

"I wouldn't tell anyone what you tell me. It's boyfriend-girl-friend confidentiality."

He finally looks at me, and his grimace has turned into a slight smirk. "I thought women always gossiped to each other about the men in their lives."

"We talk about you boys, but no sensitive information is leaked."

"So you lot are secret agents?"

"Glad you're feeling less anxious. You wouldn't be teasing me otherwise."

He palms my ass. "But I'm being serious. You are a sexy spy, ferreting out all my secrets."

"Then maybe you'll answer the question I asked you on the day we met."

Nick groans. "I think I know which one that is. Let's go inside so we can talk in private."

We start to head for the house, but someone shouts, "No time for a shag, Nick. The groomsmen have a sacred duty to perform, and you're our leader."

"Right now?" Nick asks as we both turn around.

I see the man speaking is Reese Dixon. He's much younger than Nick, but they share the same wicked sense of humor.

"Yes, right now," Reese shouts.

Nick looks at me. "I swear I did not plan this just so I could get out of answering your question."

"I know that. Go, have fun with the other boys. It's your brother's big day, after all."

"By 'sacred duty' Reese means we'll be mercilessly teasing Rick until five minutes before the ceremony starts."

"Yeah, I figured." I kiss his cheek. "See you after the ceremony."

The second Nick walks away, the American Wives Club swarms me. While the men have taken off to who-knows-where, their wives insist we all accompany the bride to a restaurant just outside town where they've reserved a back room for our pre-wedding revelry. The bride and groom decided not to have a rehearsal dinner last night since Nick and I couldn't get away in time for that. Richard and Maddie swore they didn't mind at all. As long as they can tie the knot, they're happy.

Instead, today the men will have their get-together, and we ladies will have ours.

The American Wives Club has invited ladies who are married but not American and a few like me who are still single. Well, unmarried. I'm with Nick now, so I don't qualify as single anymore. I wind up talking to every woman in attendance, though the conversations aren't long. The bride will need time to get ready, so our party is limited to one hour. The food is delicious, and the company is top-notch. Though I've spent only a short time with these women, I already adore them. Maddie Solberg and the wives of the Dixon men spend the most time with me, and I hear all about the crazy things they've done.

"Aren't you going to tell Siobhan about what Richard, Nick, and Alex did?" Rika Dixon, wife of Dane, asks when Maddie finishes telling me a story about when she and Rick stayed on a reclusive author's private island.

"I don't know what you mean," Maddie says, batting her eyelashes in a phony expression of innocence.

"Siobhan should be warned, don't you think?" Rika wags a finger at Maddie, who's her older sister. "Or are you in cahoots with them this time?"

"Cahoots?" Maddie snickers. "I can honestly say I have never heard you use that word before."

Rika rolls her eyes. "Are you going to tell Siobhan, or do I have to do it?"

"Oh no, neither of us is telling her anything. Not yet. Richard made me cross his heart and swear a solemn oath." She feigns innocent confusion, touching her finger to her lips. "Wait, maybe I was supposed to cross *my* heart."

"Uh-huh." Rika shakes her head. "I knew it. Rick has been drugging you so you'll be his sex slave. That's why you can't remember anything."

"Oh please. You're the one who can't be away from your husband for more than thirty seconds. Dane must have drugged you, or maybe he got Kirsty MacTaggart to cast a spell on you."

Kirsty is among the woman at our little shindig, and I spoke to her earlier. She's from the Scots contingent, and she's an avowed Wiccan who owns a metaphysical shop. Kirsty told me about how Alex Thorne arranged for her ex-boyfriend to make a surprise visit at her cousin Jack's wedding.

If Alex is conspiring with Nick and Richard…

Oh, I could be in trouble.

My phone rings, and I see it's Nick calling. "Excuse me, girls. Nick needs to hear my voice."

"Aw, that's so sweet," Maddie says, and I don't think she's being sarcastic. "Hunter men need lots of cuddling and sweet-talking. Just think, soon you and I could be sisters-in-law."

I just met Nick a month ago, so she's jumping the gun big time. But I don't have a chance to tell her that because I rush out of the banquet hall and down the hallway that leads to the restrooms. It's the quietest place to take a call.

"How's the bachelor party going?" I ask Nick when I answer the phone.

"It's not a bachelor party. You'll be happy to know we're having a laid-back do in the backyard of Chance Dixon's house."

"We girls are in a restaurant, but we're just gabbing."

"That's pretty much what we're doing too. Don't let on I told you that, though. Can't have anyone's male pride getting wounded."

"Okay. I'll tell Maddie you've got a stripper giving Rick a lap dance."

"Hmm, I'm feeling the need to spank you later."

"We haven't tried that yet. Maybe I'll spank you too."

Nick chuckles. "I was right. When we first met, I could tell you had a naughty streak hidden under all that tweed."

"You bring out my wild side." He really does, and I love it. "Did you have a legitimate, wedding-related reason for calling?"

"Not directly related. But there is something I needed to tell you. Hang on a minute."

I hear muffled voices, like Nick is holding his hand over the phone while he talks to someone. Scuffling noises follow, and I have no idea what's going on.

"Hello, love, are you feeling randy today?"

Yeah, I recognize that voice. I can't help it. I burst out laughing. "Did Nick put you up to this, Richard? I could tell he was plotting something."

"Yes, he did." Richard sighs and, while clearly holding the phone away from his face, he shouts, "I told you she wouldn't fall for it. Maddie didn't either. You can't fool a woman who has a PhD."

More scuffling. Then another male voice says, "Well, Siobhan, are you gagging for a kiss?"

"No, Reese, but thanks for the offer."

He chuckles and shouts to Nick, "Sorry, mate, no dice. You Hunters shouldn't marry women who have higher IQs than you."

"Like Arden isn't cleverer than you by tenfold," another voice shouts, one I recognize as Chance Dixon.

"I know she is," Reese replies, "which is why I don't try to trick her."

After another scuffling noise, Nick comes on the line again. "Sorry. That was a stupid joke."

"Do I get to hear Alex Thorne whisper dirty sweet nothings in my ear too? That must be what Maddie was talking about when she said you, Rick, and Alex did something to her."

"Yes, that's what we did. Only that was an in-person experiment, not over the phone."

"Why did you want to fool me?"

"Not sure. It seemed like the thing to do. Sorry."

"Stop apologizing. It was hilarious."

He hesitates while other voices chatter in the background. "How did you know who was who? You met these blokes today."

"I've always had a good ear for voices."

"That's impressive. If we ever get married, I'll be the luckiest man on earth."

Married. He said that word. In reference to us. And I'm not freaked out by it.

The sound of heels clicking on the floor draws my attention to the other end of the hall.

Rika Dixon trots up to me. "Time to go. It's get-the-bride-ready time."

"Sorry, Nick, I have to go," I say into the phone.

"I do too. See you at the church."

The other ladies are filing out of the banquet hall, so Rika and I follow them. In a little while, I'll get to see Nick in a fancy suit. Even thinking about that sends a hot, liquid shiver racing through me.

Oh yes, I will need to have sex with Nick the second the wedding is over.

Chapter Seventeen

My brother is getting married in fifteen minutes. I'd assumed Richard would never take the time to meet a woman, much less fall in love and get married. He was always obsessed with work, with keeping our father's publishing company going strong and ensuring Edward Hunter's legacy didn't crumble to dust. Sure, that's a noble aspiration. But Rick always took his job too seriously.

Now, he plans to take a holiday in the Caribbean. Again. Voluntarily. He and Maddie will honeymoon on the private island owned by Sir Dexter Armstrong-Hill, the reclusive author who has become my brother's mate.

Rick has changed. But have I?

Since I've become embroiled in a scandal, I think the answer is no. I haven't become a better man.

We're in a small room in the church, which I've been told is the minister's office, and I'm trying to help my brother with something called a "cravat," which he insists on wearing instead of a bow tie. My fingers keep slipping. That's what happens when you struggle to tie slippery cloth that doesn't want to be tied.

"You'll have to go without the cravat," I tell Richard. "It won't work. If you wanted to dress Victorian, you should have dug up a

Victorian gent from his grave so he could explain how to tie this bloody thing."

"Go get Alex. He knows how to do it."

Oddly, I can believe Alex Thorne knows all about Victorian clothing. He's an archaeologist, after all. Maybe he's dug up fossilized cravats.

I rush into the hallway and almost collide with Chance Dixon. His two brothers and Alex are with him.

"What are you four doing out here?" I ask. "The groomsmen are supposed to wait at the altar, but Reese and Alex are meant to be in the pews with their wives."

Chance claps me on the shoulder. "Relax, Nick, we'll get to our assigned places in a few minutes."

I glance at Alex. "Richard thinks you know how to tie a Victorian cravat."

"That's because I do."

"Well, get your arse in there and help him. I'm useless when it comes to that historical rubbish." I see the Dixons and Alex have their cravats on already. "Ah, I need your help too."

Alex fixes my tie-like whatsit and then heads into the office to help Rick.

I look down the hallway and see Siobhan talking to Rika Dixon. They're standing just outside the entrance to the chapel. Their conversation ends, and Rika walks through the doors.

Siobhan notices me and smiles. Then she sweeps her gaze over me from head to toe, her smile turning sexy as hell. She licks her lips with one long, slow glide of her tongue. When she meets my gaze again, she fans herself with her hand and forms an O shape with her mouth. She even pretends she might faint.

I wink.

She winks back, then walks into the chapel.

I understand why Rick and Maddie wanted to get married in old-fashioned clothing, but I'm sure Siobhan is wondering what on earth it's all about.

Alex emerges from the office. "Time for everyone to find his place."

He and the Dixons hurry into the chapel.

I know Alex meant everyone needs to find his place in the wedding, as in taking their positions at the altar or in the pews. But his words make me wonder. Have I found my place in life? I thought I had, but the scandal I've gotten sucked into makes me feel like I haven't found my place at all.

But with Siobhan, I don't feel that way.

Richard walks out of the office and tugs his long-tailed jacket like it needs straightening. "Let's go."

If he's nervous, he's hiding it very well. Rick has always been good at that. I'm the "see it on his face" kind of man. Sometimes I wish I could disguise my feelings.

But not with Siobhan.

I accompany my brother down the aisle, and we take our assigned positions at the altar. I can't help searching the crowd for Siobhan—and it is a crowd, for sure. Richard has a lot of friends and colleagues. Even the notorious recluse, Sir Dexter Armstrong-Hill, has come to watch my brother marry Madeleine Solberg. He did play a part in the two of them getting together, but I hadn't thought he would want to leave his tropical island. Dexter's daughter, Ilsa, has come with him.

All the guests are here. It's time for the bride's entrance.

The music starts, and the bridesmaids begin their trek to the altar. Rika is the matron of honor, of course, since she's Maddie's sister. The other bridesmaids are Elena and Arden, the wives of Chance and Reese Dixon.

I finally find Siobhan in the crowd. She smiles and gives me the thumbs-up sign, then blows me a kiss. I can't catch that kiss, though. I have a job to do here, even if I have no clue what I'm meant to do other than keep track of the rings.

The music stops, then starts up again with the wedding march.

Maddie ambles toward the altar wearing a lacy Victorian gown, her hair piled on her head in a loose style that suits her.

She's beautiful, but I can't stop my gaze from wandering back to Siobhan. I see her, but she's focused on the couple about to pledge their eternal devotion to each other or whatever bollocks it is. That's the old me talking. Watching Siobhan's face, and seeing the tears that gather in her eyes, I don't feel like marriage is rubbish. I get a strange pang in my chest, but I like it.

And yes, I get choked up when Rick and Maddie recite their vows while gazing lovingly into each other's eyes. Tears roll down her cheeks, and even Rick's eyes glisten like he might cry.

Is this all it takes to make a grown man cry? Throw an incredible woman into his path, let him fall in love, and…tears at the altar.

When Richard kisses Maddie, the entire crowd erupts in cheers and clapping. Several people whistle. Instead of throwing rice as the happy couple exits the church, everyone tosses white rose petals at them while they climb into a limousine. Rick and Maddie wanted to ride to the reception venue alone.

Oh yes, I'm sure my brother plans to consummate the marriage in that car.

Siobhan and I carpool with Reese, Arden, and Bennett Montague, my mate and employee. I haven't seen Ben in a while, but I don't get the chance to catch up with him during the car ride. Siobhan is sandwiched between us in the backseat, but I don't talk to her either. Reese insists on chatting to us the entire time, despite the fact he's driving.

I learn everything I didn't need to know about Reese and Arden's adventures in the advertising world. She's a freelance factchecker, but Reese's wife goes with him on every business trip and for his extended stays at the New York headquarters of Bonsoir Beauty Inc., where he works for Arden's grandmother. She's a billionaire, naturally, like Evan MacTaggart. Several MacTaggarts, as well as Chance and Dane Dixon, are millionaires or possibly multimillionaires. So is Richard.

Am I the only person I know who isn't rolling in money?

Siobhan and I separate from the others once we've climbed out of the car. We hold hands as we enter the reception venue. It's a park with a gazebo and lots of tables set up around that. Someone has created an L-shaped table in the gazebo by taking a shorter one and pushing it widthwise up against a longer table. The bride and groom have the shorter table to themselves. I'm sitting closest to Richard while Rika sits closest to Maddie. I can still talk to my brother despite the table between us. Siobhan is right beside me, wearing a lovely modern frock. It's blue, and the dress molds to her torso and hips before flaring out into a skirt that flounces around her calves when she walks.

Maybe I'm biased—all right, I am one hundred percent biased—but I think she's the most beautiful woman here. The most beautiful woman, full stop.

We do the speeches bollocks, and yes, I spice up my speech with a bit of innuendo, but only because I know Rick doesn't mind. He's used to me after forty years. More than that, actually, considering we've been together since the womb. I do, of course, conclude my speech with a saccharine statement about how perfect he and Maddie are for each other. It might not be all saccharine rubbish, though. I do believe Rick and Maddie belong together. I've never seen two people better suited for each other, or two people who are more in love.

Rick and Maddie cut the cake but don't stuff it into each other's mouths. They feed each other with all the grace of true Victorians while a band plays old songs from the forties and fifties. I guess the Victorian theme doesn't extend to the music.

During dinner, Siobhan leans close to whisper in my ear. "You look so good in that suit. I'm already wet for you."

"You can't want to have sex at my brother's wedding."

"Are you saying Nick Hunter, the man who let me give him a blow job in my office, is afraid to get it on at a family event?"

"There are children here. Maybe we should wait until we get back to Mum and Dad's house." What am I saying? I've never turned down the chance to shag a woman anytime, anywhere. So I press my mouth to hers. "Forget what I just said. After the bride and groom have their first dance, I am going to fuck you wherever you want."

"Good." She eats another bite of her food before asking, "What's with the Victorian outfits you guys are wearing? I wanted to ask somebody about that, but there wasn't time before the ceremony. Too much prep going on."

I'm about to explain when Rick stands up and announces, "It's time for our first dance as husband and wife."

He leads Maddie out to the open, grassy area where a temporary dance floor has been created with polished wood planks. Once the bride and groom have danced for a minute or so, other couples begin to join them. I lead Siobhan over there so we can share a dance, but then we both wind up dancing with other people—for too long. I want to hold my date in my arms, not chat to Arden and Rika and several Scots lasses.

Finally, I seize control of Siobhan. That means I grab her hand the second the music stops because I know it will start up again any second and some other bloke will sweep her away. I guide her off the dance floor and back into the gazebo. Rick and Maddie are there, alone, feeding each other wedding cake.

They're sitting at the long table, so Siobhan and I take seats opposite them.

"Siobhan has a burning question for you," I tell Richard. "She wants to know what's with all the Victorian rubbish."

"It's not rubbish, Nick," Richard says.

"Just tell her the story."

He turns to Siobhan. "When Maddie and I first met, we were invited to stay on a private island belonging to Sir Dexter Armstrong-Hill, the Nobel Prize-winning author. He insisted we arrive in Victorian dress because Dex loves to have fun with his guests." My brother gazes adoringly at his bride. "The time we spent on the island changed our lives. That's why we wanted to dress this way for the wedding."

I shake my head. "Honestly, Rick, you told the story better the first time I heard it."

Siobhan elbows me in the side. "Don't harass him. That was a great story, Richard. Very romantic."

My brother raises his brows at me. "Should we book this venue for you while we're here? You need to schedule it at least two months in advance."

"Book the venue for what?" I ask.

He grins. "Your wedding, of course."

"That's not funny, Rick. Siobhan and I have only known each other for a month."

"I needed slightly less than two weeks to realize I love Maddie."

"Yes, but I'm sure you thought about it for weeks before you told her, and you didn't sleep with her until after that. I'm the one who rushes into things, like having sex with a woman a few days after we've met, before I've even taken her on a real date."

Richard and Maddie glance at each other, sharing a strange look. Maddie bites her lip.

My brother shrugs. "Should we…"

His wife nods. "Yeah, I think we should."

"You two are sickeningly adorable," I say. "Reading each other's thoughts now? I might need an insulin injection to survive the sweetness."

Rick clears his throat and fidgets in his seat. "Maddie and I slept together on the day we met. I talked her into a one-night stand and left while she was still asleep. I didn't even know her name until…"

"He came back for me in the morning," Maddie says. "We introduced ourselves, and the rest is history."

I stare at my brother, speechless for a long moment. "You had a one-night stand? Everyone thinks you're the responsible one."

"We're both responsible, Nick. No one thinks you're immature, though we all know you can be impulsive at times."

Yes, I can be. But how am I meant to reconcile the Richard I know with the man who seduced sweet Madeleine on a tropical island and didn't bother to ask her name? Well, at least now I feel better about sleeping with Siobhan after a few days.

"It's still too early to start planning the wedding," I say. "That means no, do not book this venue for the reception."

There's no way I can convince Rick or Maddie that I'm not marrying Siobhan, is there?

So I stand up and offer her my hand. "Siobhan, let me introduce you to another friend of mine."

Chapter Eighteen

Siobhan

What other friend?" I ask as Nick drags me past the makeshift dance floor and toward the tables set up on the grass. He seems like he needs to get away from his brother and his sister-in-law, and I think it's because Richard mentioned the possibility of marriage. Yeah, it's much too early to talk about that. But Nick didn't need to act quite so horrified by the suggestion, did he?

"You weren't properly introduced in the car," Nick says. "So it's time for you to meet Bennett. He works for me at the spa, but he's also a good friend."

"Was he the mystery man in the limo? I wondered why he didn't speak."

"Reese wouldn't bloody shut up, that's why."

We reach a table where one man sits alone, sipping from a bottle of beer.

"There you are," Nick says, gesturing for me to sit down.

I take a seat, and Nick settles into the chair next to mine.

Nick's friend sets his bottle down and glances back and forth between us. "What's up, boss?"

"This is Siobhan Griffin," Nick says. "She's my, ah, girlfriend. And she's also a mathematics professor at a university in America. Siobhan, this is Bennett Montague, one of my best mates and one of my best employees too."

"Nice to meet you," I say to Bennett. "So you're a massage therapist like Nick?"

"That's right." He grins and winks. "Nick doesn't get to have all the fun, you know."

My boyfriend rolls his eyes. "Ben specializes in massage for physical therapy. Most of his clients are elderly or injured."

"I did have that hot gymnast client."

"Who was married and not at all interested in you, Ben." Nick gestures toward me though he still speaks to his friend. "Why don't you tell Siobhan who you are. She'll be enthralled and honored."

"You're a cheeky sod, you know that?" Bennett fidgets and screws up his mouth, like he sat on a pebble or a pin. "Maybe another time. Let's not ruin a great party by making it about me."

"All right, relax. I'm the one in the papers, not you. Remember?"

"Your situation isn't as bad as you think, Nick." Bennett stands and offers his hand to me over the table. "May I have this dance, Ms. Griffin?"

"She's Dr. Griffin," Nick says.

I get up and slip my hand into Bennett's. "Call me Siobhan. And yes, I would love to dance with you."

"My mates call me Ben. I'd like it if you would too."

"Thank you, Ben."

He escorts me onto the dance floor, and we assume the usual position, not quite ballroom quality but good enough for a wedding. I see Richard and Maddie dancing too, but she has her cheek on his shoulder and her body pressed against him. I'd love to dance with Nick that way, but he kept it chaste, almost professional, when we danced. He seems nervous, though I can't figure out why. Maybe it's the scandal that's threatening his livelihood. He must be thinking about it a lot more now that he's come home to where the scandal caught fire.

Maybe that's why we're staying at his parents' house instead of wherever he lives. I've never asked if he has an apartment or a house. We've talked about a lot of things, but asking where he lives never occurred to me.

"How did you meet Nick?" I ask Bennett while we traverse the dance floor.

"Through the Dixons." He veers us away from Richard and Maddie, who seem so engrossed in each other that they're not paying attention to anything else. "I met Reese Dixon during our first year at uni. He was studying business, and I was working on my qualifying law degree. Anyway, Richard Hunter is best mates with Chance Dixon, so I met the twins when Reese invited me to his birthday at his parents' house. I've been mates with all of them ever since."

"It's great that you boys have stayed friends for so long." I hesitate, then ask, "If you planned on becoming a lawyer, how did you end up as a massage therapist?"

"Turns out I hate all that legal rubbish. After three years of having my nose buried in the law so I could get my degree, I'd had enough. I never became a solicitor."

"Why did you finish your law degree if you hated it? Couldn't you switch majors?"

"I'm sure I could have, but my parents insisted I had to become a solicitor." He sighs and shuts his eyes briefly. "I disappointed them. Didn't mean to, but I just couldn't commit my life to the law."

"How long have you worked for Nick?"

"Five years. He encouraged me to go for the qualification course, and he let me watch him at work, with his clients' permission, so I could get a feel for the job. As soon as I finished the course, he hired me. I've taken more training since, to learn about massage as rehab for athletes." He glances toward where Nick is still sitting at the table, though now he's talking to Jack MacTaggart, the Scottish psychologist. Ben swerves his gaze back to me. "Nick has been like a big brother to me. I owe him a lot."

Maybe I should be surprised by the way Nick helped his friend find a new career, but I'm not. He cares about other people. Once I'd gotten over the shock of how much I lust for him, I quickly realized he is the sweetest man I've ever met. He never pushed me to sleep with him. He's never pushed me to make our secret relationship a public one.

He's a gentleman—with a wicked streak.

And I love that about him.

"I've been so rude," I tell Bennett. "I asked you all those questions without thinking about whether you wanted to be grilled."

"You're not grilling me," he says with a smile. "I've commandeered Nick's girlfriend. This is a first for me, so you can go on asking me as many questions as you like. I'm waiting for Nick to rush over here and shove me out of the way."

"I don't think he'll do that. And hey, you can ask me questions too."

"All right. How did you meet Nick?"

Considering that we have to keep our relationship hush-hush, at least when we're in Vallefrio, I probably shouldn't tell Ben our story. But they're friends, so I don't think Nick will mind. He trusts this man enough not only to be friends with him, but also to hire him as an employee.

So I tell Bennett the slightly abridged version of how I met Nick.

"That sounds like Nick," Ben says. "Flirting with his teacher. I bet he did that the first time he went to uni too."

"Probably. Flirtation is like breathing to him. It's a natural reflex."

"He hasn't even looked at another woman since he's been here with you."

I doubt he's looked at anyone else back in Vallefrio either. Why I believe that, I have no idea. But I feel it's the truth. Nick Hunter might be an outrageous flirt, but he's a one-woman man.

Do I want to stay his one woman after the semester ends?

The song winds down, and Bennett kisses my hand. "Thank you for permitting me to dance with you, Siobhan."

"It was my pleasure, Bennett."

He ambles over to Maddie and asks the bride for a dance.

I rejoin Nick at the little table and reclaim my seat beside him.

"Why didn't you dance with anyone while I was gone?" I ask.

He taps his finger on the water glass he still has his hand wrapped around and keeps his gaze downcast. "Had enough of dancing with other women. I was waiting for you."

"I hope it didn't bother you that I danced with your friend. Honestly, I assumed you would get out there too and have a whirl with one of the many ladies in attendance."

He shrugs, still gazing at his glass. "I only want to hold you in my arms now."

"Oh, Nick, I'm sorry. I should've asked you before I—"

"Siobhan, it's your right to dance with whoever you want." He lifts his gaze to mine. "I don't expect you to be glued to me for the rest of your life."

But maybe I want us to be glued to each other, permanently. The idea makes me feel…warm and fluttery.

"Please dance with me," I say. "Hold me in your arms, Nick."

He blinks once, slowly, like I've surprised him.

But then something behind me snares his attention, and he squints at whatever it is. His lips tighten, then he groans and slumps against his chair.

"What's wrong?" I ask.

He nods toward whatever he saw past my shoulder.

I twist around to glance in that direction. All I see is a group of women having an animated conversation, smiling and laughing, clinking their champagne glasses. The women in the group include the wives of the Dixons—Rika, Elena, Arden, and Jessica—as well as the bride, Maddie, and the wives of several Scots. They keep glancing in our direction, but I don't see why Nick should be annoyed by that.

"Why do you care that those ladies are having a good time?" I ask Nick.

"Because I know what they're doing." He rubs his forehead. "The official meeting of the American Wives Club is in session."

Chapter Nineteen

Nick

Siobhan stares at me for a moment like she can't comprehend why I've slouched down in my chair or why I'm holding a hand up to shield my face from the group of women who keep looking at me from across the lawn. Then she finally asks, "Why do you care if those ladies are having a meeting of their informal club?"

"I told you. It's because I know what they're about."

"Which is what?"

"Meddling."

Siobhan met the American Wives Club earlier, but I don't know if anyone explained to her what those nosy women like to do as their primary hobby. Well, it's more like their life's mission. I love them all—like sisters, not like I want to shag them—but sometimes they go so far overboard that they might need life preservers. In their zeal to ensure every couple finds a "happily ever after," as those women call it, sometimes they engage in tactics that border on harassment. All right, it's not quite that bad. But those women need to have more babies, strictly to keep them too busy to "help" me.

And that's what they're conspiring about right now. I know it is.

"What are they meddling with?" Siobhan asks.

"My life."

"To what end?"

I squirm in my chair and try to slump down farther, since I've caught Emery MacTaggart, the ring leader of the American Wives gang, watching me with too much interest. "They think every man needs to have a wife."

"But you don't want one."

"Maybe I do, maybe I don't. How am I meant to find out when they're poking their pretty little noses into my life?"

"Lighten up, Nick. They're nice people, not a swarm of killer bees."

I grunt. "Depends on what they're up to."

"Let me go find out."

Before I can stop her, Siobhan jumps up and marches straight over to the American Wives Club. She smiles and inserts herself into their conversation, though the other women don't seem to mind her cheerful intrusion. They welcome her with open arms—literally, since most of them hug her.

One woman separates from the crowd and approaches me.

Rika Dixon sits down on the chair Siobhan had vacated. She smiles and pats my thigh. "Don't worry, Nick, this won't hurt a bit."

"What won't hurt? I thought you lot were meddling in my love life, not scheduling a root canal for me."

She laughs. "Oh sweetie, we want to help. That's why we're plotting the most expedient ways to force you to do whatever we want. Brainwashing has been discussed. So has spellcasting, since we do have a witch on the premises. Ooh, and Maddie suggested we could slip some oysters into your meals."

"I hate oysters."

"Yeah, Richard told her that."

For a second or two, I freeze up like the temperature has dropped a hundred degrees in the span of a heartbeat. "Richard did what? He couldn't have been..."

"Participating in the meddling?" Rika waves her hand in a dismissive gesture. "You silly goose, your brother is an active and willing participant."

"You lot must've slipped a mind-altering drug into his tea." I freeze again, though not as solidly as before. "Did you say spellcasting?"

"Mm-hm." Rika pats my thigh again. "But I was kidding. Kirsty MacTaggart is a Wiccan, but she doesn't have magical powers. Now, about you…"

"There is no 'about me.' I don't need you lovely but insane women poking your noses into my life."

"Oh, it's too late, honey. We're already poking."

My gaze flies to Siobhan, who's laughing with the other American women. What are they saying to her? About me?

"What do you mean you're already poking?" I ask carefully.

"Don't worry. We're starting with your other problem, then we'll move on to helping you and Siobhan."

My other problem?

"No, Rika," I say as emphatically as I can while I'm still slouched in a chair. "I do not want or need your help. That goes for every member of your barmy club."

"Told you, it's too late. The meddling has begun. In fact, it started months ago."

Bloody perfect. They've dedicated months to plotting a way to marry me off.

I straighten in my chair and squint at her. "Why are you over here telling me this? I thought meddling was meant to be secret."

Rika grins and punches my arm. "I'm the official ambassador to Nick Hunter."

"Am I a country now? I don't need an ambassador, not even a beautiful one."

"Thank you for the compliment, Nick. You are such a sweetie."

I throw my head back and groan. "Why are you doing this?"

"Because I'm your ambassador," she says like I'm a very slow-witted child. "And because I love you."

Can't help it. I smirk and say, "Does Dane know you love me? He seems like the sort who would dismember my body and dump it in the Thames if he found out how you feel about me."

"Ha-ha. You know I meant I love you as a friend." She glances at something behind me and breaks into a broad smile. "Hi, honey, are you here to help me get Nick fixed up?"

Dane Dixon stops beside my chair and pushes his hands into his trouser pockets. "Rika, I thought we agreed you wouldn't be Nick's ambusher."

"It's ambassador, not ambusher." Rika gives her husband a wry look. "Honestly, Dane, you've been right there with us in the Save Nick Hunter campaign."

Save me? I'm not that bad off. Am I?

When I look at Dane, he bows his head and clears his throat.

Oh yes, he has thrown in with those meddling women for sure.

"Even Rick is on board," Rika says. "Maddie talked him into it, but now he thinks it's a fabulous idea."

"What is a fabulous idea?" I ask.

"You'll find out."

I glance at Dane. "Did you know your wife loves me?"

He chuckles. "I know everything about Rika."

Siobhan returns to our table and eyes the three of us with an odd expression. "Looks like I missed something."

"Yes, you did," I say as I push up out of my chair and claim her hand. "Rika loves me, and Dane is plotting revenge."

"No, I am not," Dane says.

Siobhan leans into me. "Do I need to fight for my man?"

I palm her arse. "Only if it involves mud wrestling in the nude."

"What about Jell-O wrestling?"

"If it's in the nude, I'm fine with any type of contact sport."

Dane smiles and shakes his head at us, then he and Rika walk away.

"We scared them off," I tell Siobhan.

She slips an arm around me. "Can we go inside now? To your bedroom?"

"Absolutely. I'm too knackered to pull off a good shag, though."

"That's okay. I'd love to just snuggle with you."

"I'd love that too."

We make our way past the gazebo, pausing to inform the bride and groom that we're leaving. Rick and Maddie don't care. They're about to sneak off themselves. Siobhan and I accompany them to the car that's waiting to whisk them away to a posh hotel in London for a two-night stay, then on Monday, they'll get whisked even farther away—to Elusion Island in the Caribbean, where they met. After a night there, they'll fly to Sir Dexter Armstrong-Hill's private island for the remainder of their honeymoon.

Dexter won't be there, though. Somehow, my brother convinced a recluse to go on a book tour to promote the first of eight new novels the cheeky codger has written.

I like Dexter. We get on well, which Rick says means I will be just like Dex when I'm his age. We do share a similar sense of humor.

After seeing the happy couple off, Siobhan and I take a taxi to my parents' house and snuggle together on the bed I slept in until I was eighteen. It feels strange to have her in my childhood room, but it also feels…right.

She lays an arm over my belly. "Do you have an apartment or house of your own?"

"Yes, I have a house in Cockshire."

"That name still sounds made up to me."

"And I still can't help that someone decided to name the town that."

"Why are we staying at your parents' place instead of yours?"

"Because my home is ground zero for that sodding scandal." I turn my face toward her to breathe in the scent of her hair. "Tomorrow, I'll take you to Cockshire and show you my business and my home. All right? If we get accosted by a horde of women who are gagging for a 'special' massage, you can't say I didn't warn you."

"I can handle it, Nick. Jeez, I deal with college kids all day long, five days a week. They're much more difficult than lustful women."

"Can we shag now? I'm feeling reinvigorated."

She laughs. "Have I ever turned down sex with you?"

"No, you're more likely to shred my clothes."

Even while I'm making love to Siobhan, I keep wondering what those American women are plotting.

Chapter Twenty

Siobhan

Nick and I borrow his brother's car for our trip to Cockshire, which is only ten minutes from Colchester. The town where Nick lives and works might have a strange name, but it's the cutest little "chocolate box village," which is what Nick says Brits call this kind of town. It has quaint cottages and quaint shops, plus beautiful scenery. We pass verdant fields hemmed in by lush trees on our way into the village, and I can't help feeling awed by the beauty of this region. I've lived in New Mexico for a long time and rarely took vacations away from home.

I think I forgot what plant life looks like.

Nick gets more anxious the closer we get to Cockshire. He grips the steering wheel tighter, and he seems to be clenching his jaw.

That idiotic scandal has upset him more than I ever realized.

As we enter the village, we drive past big brick houses with brick walls that encompass them. Some are low walls, but others are quite tall. Every house has shrubs or hedges, and flowering trees and bushes.

"It's beautiful here," I say. "Are we going straight to your house, or stopping off at your spa first?"

He twists his hands around the wheel like he's trying to strangle it. "I thought I'd show you my business first."

"Sounds good." I lay a hand on his arm. "Relax, Nick. I don't see any rampaging mob of lust-crazed women. No villagers with pitchforks and torches either."

"I know," he says on a long sigh. "But I have no idea what people round here think of me anymore."

"They used to like you, right?"

"Yes. I think so, at any rate."

"Come on, you're a pillar of the community."

A laugh splutters out of him, but it seems more panicked than amused. "Pillar? Me? You've got me confused with my brother and my parents. I'm a massage therapist."

"Wow, you have quite the inferiority complex, don't you?"

"No, I—I'm not as accomplished as the rest of my family."

"I know your dad started a publishing company," I say, "and now Richard owns it. What does your mom do?"

"She dedicated her life to raising me and Rick and taking care of the household. She's a member of the WI, and she volunteers for various charities." He tries to strangle the steering wheel again. "So yes, she's as impressive as Dad and Rick."

"Never heard of the WI. What is that?"

"Women's Institutes. Ladies get together to hear speeches or learn how to cook or craft various kinds of…things you cook or craft. I've never been to a WI meeting, so I can't give you the details."

"That's okay." I watch his face while he steers the car around a corner onto a quaint street lined with various kinds of businesses—a solicitor's office, an estate agent's office, an antiques shop, and more. "Why do you feel like you're not as good as your family?"

He winces just a touch, but I can't tell if it's discomfort or simply because he's concentrating on parking the car along the street. Parallel parking makes me nervous, but I wouldn't have thought Nick would feel that way. He's confident, and if not fearless, at least willing to take risks like going back to school at forty years old. So that expression is probably discomfort about my questions.

"We're here," he says and climbs out of the car.

Before I can open my door, he rushes around to my side and opens it for me. He even offers me his hand to help me climb out.

"Thank you, Nick," I say. "You really are an old-fashioned gentleman."

"You're confusing me with Richard. I'm the man who put his 'big feet' on your desk and flirted with you shamelessly."

"Sure, but I'm the woman who literally ripped the shirt off your body."

A smile tugs at the corners of his mouth but doesn't quite form. "Sometimes I don't know why you're here with me. A summer affair doesn't obligate you to meet my family."

"Who said it's a summer affair? We're dating, Nick, remember?"

He lifts his shoulders in a halfhearted shrug.

I want to talk about this more, to make him feel better. Seeing him anxious and full of… Well, it's not quite self-loathing. But he does have some self-esteem issues.

"Do you want to go inside?" he asks, waving toward the building behind us.

"Yes, of course." I finally turn to look at the building, and I can't help smiling. "Nick's Nirvana? No wonder everyone thinks you give happy endings here."

"It's a day spa, not a brothel."

"Sorry, I was making a joke. A bad one, apparently." I slip my hand into his. "Show me your baby."

"You're wanting me to hold a mirror up to your face?"

Snarky, flirtatious Nick is back. I'm glad for that, but I still need to convince him to talk to me, seriously talk to me, about why he thinks his brother and his parents are more worthy of admiration than he is.

I bump my shoulder into him. "Show me your business, Nick. That's your baby."

"No, it's my livelihood."

He pulls a set of keys out of his pocket and leads me to the front door of the spa. The words Nick's Nirvana are painted on the door in an elaborate, sprawling script. The same words appear on the big sign above our heads, the one affixed to the building. Both signs also list some of the services offered here—deep tissue massage, sports massage, underwater massage, steam rooms, facials, acupuncture, and Reiki. The signs also say "and so much more." Could that be what convinced people Nick is a gigolo? The horrible woman who started the rumor set things in motion, but then townspeople's imaginations took over and they wondered what the "and so much more" means.

That's no excuse, though. Ruining a man's life is unforgivable.

But this village looks like such a nice place.

Nick unlocks the door and ushers me inside.

The walls are painted in soothing shades of light blue and yellow accented with pale rose and soft green. Images of leaves and flower petals form a border along the tops of the walls and snake down here and there as if they're reaching out to the chairs positioned beneath them. We walk past the front desk and through a doorway into a hall.

"These are the relaxation suites," Nick tells me. "I'd first thought to call them treatment rooms, but that didn't sound welcoming."

"Yeah, 'relaxation suites' is nicer."

"Each room has a specific purpose." He points to doorways as we pass them. "That's a Reiki suite. There's a massage room that can be used for any type of massage, except underwater. We have a special place for that."

While I follow Nick and listen to his explanations of each suite's purpose, I become more and more convinced that he is just as intelligent, accomplished, and determined as his brother and his parents. Nick has created a thriving business that offers all kinds of options in an environment that's designed to soothe. Upstairs, I see even more relaxation suites.

Nick leads me into his office. "This is where I do all the bloody annoying paperwork and accounting rubbish."

"You call it rubbish, but everything you've shown me and told me proves that you are an impressive businessman. You built this place from the ground up and made it successful."

"It was sheer luck."

"Bullshit, Nick." I move in front of him and grasp both his hands. "You did this. You created a thriving business. Don't downplay what you've done here."

"I'm a massage therapist, not a doctor or a mathematics professor."

"Do you think I'm smarter than you? I'm not. Being good at math doesn't make me better than you or anyone." I study his face, trying to puzzle out why he feels the need to downplay his accomplishments. "Did you decide to finish your degree so you could prove you're worthy?"

He veers his gaze away from mine and clears his throat. "Possibly."

I wrap my arms around his neck. "Oh Nick, you are worthy. Not having a degree doesn't make you any less accomplished or any less intelligent than Richard or your dad."

He bows his head. "Mostly, I wanted to get away from England for a while, because of the scandal. But deep down, I think I also wanted to show my family I'm…not a useless chancer who only cares about seducing women."

"They already know that. You have nothing to prove."

"My academic record is 'adequate.' You said so yourself."

"I'm sorry I told you that. I only said it because you knocked me off-kilter the moment we met. You're sexy, funny, smart, and flirtatious. I'm not used to being attracted to someone at first sight. Don't think it's ever happened to me before."

"You like me because I give you incredible sex."

I tickle his neck. "No, I like you because you're Nicholas T. Hunter, world's oldest college student."

He exhales a long, resigned sigh that makes his shoulders sag. "I suppose that's better than being Nick the Gigolo."

Though I want to ask him more questions, I feel like I should hold off on that—but only for a little while. "You've shown me your business. Will you show me your home now?"

"Of course."

He leads me downstairs and out of the building. Just as he's locking the door, a woman rushes up to us.

"Are you open today?" she asks, her eyes large and darting around like she's excited or maybe on drugs.

"No, I'm afraid not," Nick says, stuffing the keys in his pocket. "We're open Monday through Saturday. If you'd like to make an appointment, please call tomorrow. Now, if you'll excuse us…"

When he tries to walk past the woman, she seizes his arm. "Don't you offer special appointments after hours?"

Her tone implies she wants the kind of "special" massage Nick does not offer.

I watch his face, the way his expression falls, and then tightens into a pained look. "Sorry, no, we don't do that. Whatever you've heard is a lie. This is a legitimate day spa."

She tugs on his arm, pressing herself closer to him. "But Georgina says—"

"That woman is a liar." Nick's tone has become sharp, and he all but snarls those words through his gritted teeth. Shutting his eyes, he lets out a miserable, groaning sigh. Then he looks at the woman again. "I'm sorry, I shouldn't have snapped at you. The truth is that Lady Prescott is mistaken about what my spa offers."

He hustles me to the car, and we don't speak as we climb in or while he starts the engine and pulls out onto the street.

That woman gapes at us until we've driven out of view of her.

I glance at Nick.

His face has become the picture of stone-cold anger.

"Are you okay?" I ask.

"Not yet, but I will be. Give me a few minutes."

I decide to do that. Whatever Nick has been through lately, I want to help him get through it—if he'll let me. And suddenly, I realize what that means. Nick is more than a lover to me. He's more than a friend too. What exactly I feel for him, I'm not quite sure yet.

But I intend to find out.

Right now, what I want to do more than anything is hunt down Georgina Prescott and give her a piece of my mind.

Chapter Twenty-One

Nick

Maybe I glare at the street ahead of me while I drive Siobhan to my home. Maybe I grip the steering wheel like I want to throttle it. And maybe I even growl under my breath a few times. Can anyone blame me? Despite her title, Georgina Prescott is no lady. She's the cow who started the rumor and forced me to flee from my homeland to find sanctuary on the other side of an ocean, on the far side of another continent.

I wish that woman would find a new hobby and give up ruining my life.

But is it ruined? Or am I wallowing in self-pity?

Siobhan will fall in love with me for sure when I'm behaving like a self-centered, whingeing arse, won't she? Not sure if I want her to love me, but it won't happen now.

I shouldn't have gotten annoyed when that woman, who I've never seen before, asked about "special" services. It's not her fault Georgina spread a vicious lie about me.

Once I've parked the car in front of my house, I hurry around to the passenger side to open the door for Siobhan and help her step out.

She smiles and kisses my cheek. "No matter what anyone else might say, I know you're a gentleman and a good person."

"I'm a walking scandal."

"No, you are not."

Siobhan Griffin is the cleverest, most centered person I've ever met. If she believes in me, maybe I should too.

The second we've walked into the house and I've shut the door, she rounds on me. "We need to finish our conversation from earlier."

"Conversation? I've already told you Georgina Prescott is a liar."

"I'm not talking about that." She glances around at the furniture in the living room. "Let's sit on the sofa and talk more about why you feel unworthy."

I can't stop a groan from rumbling out of me. "Must we? I'm knackered."

"No, you're avoiding the issue."

All right, maybe she has a point. But can anyone blame me? Talking about my narcissistic feelings of inadequacy isn't the kind of conversation I want to have with Siobhan. I'd much rather whisper dirty things in her ear. And I did bring that little surprise for her...

I pull her close. "How would you like a 'special' massage?"

"You got upset when that woman on the street asked for one of those."

"That's different. You're different."

She drags one fingertip across my bottom lip. "In that case, I'd love a 'special' massage. Later. Right now, will you answer one question for me?"

I want to groan again, but I'm an adult, not a teenager who can get away with acting like a spoiled child. Or maybe teenagers can't get away with that. My mother never would've stood for it.

Adult behavior it is, then. *Bugger.*

Resisting the urge to sigh or groan, I say, "All right. Ask me."

"Why did you quit college one semester away from graduating?"

"Please, any question but that one. The answer will make me sound narcissistic."

"No, it won't. Trust me."

Do I trust her? Yes. I didn't realize how much until this moment, when she asked the question I never want to answer. But for her, I will.

I guide her to the sofa and sit down, then wait while she settles in beside me. "When we were growing up, Rick and I were very close and did everything together. We even went on double dates and attended the same university. We shared a room in the residence hall too. Rick and I were inseparable for most of our lives, but at university, things changed."

"In what way?"

"Richard took all the intellectual classes, literature and things like that. I focused on business and management." Am I slouching? Bollocks, I am. Pushing myself up straighter gives me a few seconds' reprieve. "Studying different fields meant we moved in different circles despite being twins and living together. It didn't happen overnight, but gradually, we sort of…moved apart."

Siobhan wriggles around until she's sideways to me with her feet tucked under her.

In that position, and dressed in casual clothes, she looks younger. I almost feel like a dirty old man who seduced a college girl. Siobhan is so…adorable.

And I find myself telling her everything. "Rick got involved in extracurricular activities like the poetry club, while I spent my free time reading business magazines and chasing girls. None of that mattered, not really. We might be physically identical, but we aren't two halves of the same person."

"I understand that. You don't need to keep going on about it."

She doesn't sound irritated. Her voice and her expression are full of empathy. We hardly know each other, but she wants to understand me and…help me.

Well, I'd much rather have her "helping" me than the American Wives Club. I love those women, but I dread whatever they might be planning for me.

"Like I said, Rick and I had grown apart, somewhat," I tell Siobhan. "But the big change happened in our last year at university. That was when our father announced Richard would inherit the publishing company when he retired, and he was grooming my brother for that role. Rick wanted to do it. He's always loved Hunter Publishing, used to hang out there every summer to watch Dad at work. I tried to do that, but I got so bloody bored."

"Okay, your dad offered Richard the company, which you didn't want. Why did that make you drop out of school?"

"It didn't, not at first." I drop my head back against the sofa and stare at the ceiling. "But I started to wonder why my father hadn't asked if I wanted to work at his company. The idea never occurred to him. Why should it? I'm the son who cares more about having fun than running a business. Like I told you before, Dad chose the right son."

"But you own a business. A successful one, with employees and everything."

What else can I do but keep staring at the ceiling? I have no idea how to explain this to her in a way that won't sound moronic. Maybe I shouldn't worry about that. If she ends our…whatever this is because I'm a pathetic idiot, at least I won't need to worry anymore about whether she'll throw me over.

Yes, don't I have a positive attitude?

Siobhan rests her cheek on my shoulder. "You can tell me, Nick. I won't think any less of you, no matter what you say."

I let out a long sigh and tell her. "Rick already had an internship lined up for after graduation. This was in the first semester of our last year at university. I had applied for several internships, but just before Christmas, I found out I hadn't gotten any of them. I'd also gone to job fairs and thought I had good prospects for getting a job if the internships didn't work out. But I found out all those opportunities had fallen through too."

"That's why you quit school."

"No, that was part of the reason." I cover my face with my hands and groan. "I told you Rick and I had grown apart somewhat during our university days. He had no idea I was dating anyone, so he never knew the girl I was in love with had thrown me over for him. She met Rick when she joined the poetry club, and the faithless cow never mentioned to my brother—my identical twin brother—that she was having sex with me."

"Then what happened?"

"One night, he stayed out until morning. When he came back to our room, he was in the best mood I'd ever seen him in. Rick said he'd met a wonderful girl, and he'd spent the night with her. Couldn't stop grinning and saying her name."

"Did you tell him she'd been your girlfriend?"

"No, he never knew. How could I tell him? He never had as much luck with women as I did. Well, until he met Maddie."

Siobhan lifts her head to look at me. "I don't understand. Why would you quit school because a stupid girl dumped you?"

"That girl, Gina, told me Rick is much better in every way than I am. If she can have a man who looks like me but isn't me, and who's as good in bed as I am, then why should she bother with me? I'm not very clever, and all she wanted was my body."

"But—"

"I know, I know. Let me finish, all right?" I sit up straighter and force myself to look at Siobhan. "I realized then that I will never be as clever or as accomplished or as good at anything as my brother. That's all right. I'm proud of Rick. He deserves everything he's got. He worked hard for it, much harder than I ever have. I sort of fell into massage therapy. I would give massages to my friends when they got sore playing sports, and to my girlfriends too. Everyone told me I should do that for a living. So I did."

"Nick, you are not less accomplished or less intelligent than your brother." She slaps a hand over my mouth when I open it to speak. "Shush, I'm not done."

She removes her hand.

And I keep my mouth shut.

"You need to tell Richard about all of that," she says. "Tell your dad too. You've been carrying this around for way too long."

"Honestly, it never bothered me until this whole 'special' massage business. Being the center of a scandal is a surefire way to flush your self-esteem down the toilet."

"You are confident. That's one of the sexiest things about you." She loops her arms around my neck and presses her lips to my ear. "You never doubt yourself when you're flirting with me or when we're having sex. Apply some of that confidence to the rest of your life. No more running away."

"Are you telling me to quit school?"

"No, I'm telling you to make sure you're in school for the right reasons, not because you think you need to prove something to your family or that silly girl Gina."

"I haven't seen or spoken to her since I left university."

"You know what I mean."

Oh yes, I know what she means. And she's right, of course. I should tell Rick and my father. I've kept this to myself for far too long, so it's time to act like a mature adult.

"Do you like your job?" she asks. "Or is that your second-choice career?"

"Maybe it started out that way, but I've come to love it." I lay a hand on her thigh. "You know how I love to make women feel good."

"You're incorrigible."

"I also make blokes feel good, but strictly in a professional capacity. The entire Cockshire cricket team relies on my massages. Those chaps play like their matches will determine the fate of the world."

"Do you play sports?"

I slide my hand up her thigh. "You're well acquainted with my particular brand of sport."

"Mm, yes. It's highly energetic and thoroughly satisfying."

"Want that massage now?"

"Maybe later. It's lunchtime now, and I'm hungry."

I get up and kiss the top of her head. "We'll call the food our first course. The second course of our meal will take place in bed."

She grabs my shirt and drags me in for a kiss.

Who cares about school? I've learned everything I need to know from Siobhan and her insatiable appetites.

Chapter Twenty-Two

Siobhan

Nick doesn't give me a "special" massage, not that afternoon. We don't have sex either. Instead, after lunch, he takes me on a tour of Essex, which is the name of the county he lives in. Though we drive through Colchester, he makes excuses for why he doesn't want to stop by his parents' house, and I decide to let him procrastinate a little longer before I lovingly push him to tell his family the real reason he left school.

I think he hasn't given me a sexy massage because he's worried by doing that, he'll somehow validate the rumor about him. Nobody will know what we do together in the privacy of his home, but I still get the feeling he worries about it. That's Nick. He's a confident, sexy, smart man who sometimes forgets that's his true nature. I hadn't known he could be vulnerable until we decided to become a couple. Knowing he has a sensitive side makes me like him even more.

In the evening, after we've enjoyed a satisfying meal, Nick leads me upstairs. He stops along the way to adjust the thermostat, seeming to turn up the temperature.

"Expecting a cold spell tonight?" I ask.

"No. But I can't have you getting a chill."

"Cold doesn't bother me. Besides, it's quite comfortable in here."

He gives me a sexy, secretive smile and continues leading me upstairs—to his bedroom, I discover.

"Sleepy already?" I ask.

"No, I'm not tired." He takes both my hands, walking forward while backing me up toward the bed, then he gently pushes me to sit down at the foot. "I have a surprise for you. But first, you'll need to be blindfolded. All right?"

"Sure." I would let him do anything to me. Maybe I should be concerned about why I feel that way, but I don't care what the reason is. It feels good.

Nick retrieves a necktie from a dresser drawer and ties it around my head, covering my eyes with the silky fabric. "Now, just sit there and wonder about what I'm doing."

"I'm already curious."

An odd sound follows, like a match being struck. I hear him moving around, and I notice that odd sound again, several times.

He grasps my shoulders. "Stand up, love. I need to get the bed ready."

"I can help."

"That would spoil the surprise." He brushes his lips over mine. "Patience, love."

He's called me "love" twice. I think he's called me that before too. It's probably just a British thing, and I shouldn't read too much into it.

I stand up with Nick's hands steadying me. There's something intensely erotic about not knowing what he has planned.

More noises follow. The rustling of fabric. The puffing of pillows. The whispering of his breaths.

God, I'm so turned on I can hardly stand it. "Are you almost done? Because I'm dying to know what you're up to."

"This is what I'm up to." His voice rumbles inches from my ear, and his hands cup my bottom. He tilts my hips forward until my body meets a hard obstacle. A long, thick, hard obstacle. "Understand?"

Oh yes, I understand now. His erection is pressed into my belly, which means he's about to give me exactly what I want.

A soft aroma wafts in the air, like sandalwood and ginger.

"Mm, that smells wonderful," I say. "Did you light scented candles?"

"Yes, I did." He rubs his cock against me. "You're a very clever woman, Siobhan. That's one of the sexiest things about you. Now, I'm going to undress you."

"While I'm blindfolded?"

"That's right. Are you ready to relinquish control to me?"

"I've already done that. You can do anything you want, Nick. I trust you."

He removes my clothes piece by piece, taking his time as he unbuttons my shirt and unzips my pants. His fingers tease my skin with every movement, and my breathing becomes faster and heavier, the weight of desire increasing every second. When he gets rid of my bra, he skims his fingers over the already stiff peaks, making me suck in a breath. But when he removes my panties, he toys with the hairs on my mound, barely touching them, the delicate touch intensifying my arousal until I'm on fire for him from head to toe.

Nick whips off the blindfold. "Lie down on the bed, on your stomach."

Though I'd been in the dark until now, the light doesn't shock my eyes. The only illumination comes from the scented candles he set up on the dresser and the bedside table. The curtains above the bed are closed, giving us total privacy.

And Nick is naked. His hard cock dances in front of his body. I can't help staring at it. His length is smooth and sleek, long but not too long, and just thick enough to make my mouth water. I've seen his cock before, but this time feels different. I never took the time to appreciate his manly parts until tonight. Nick Hunter has the most beautiful dick I've ever seen, and I can't wait to have him inside me again.

"On the bed, Siobhan," he says. "Or I'll toss you onto it."

He's smirking, but I know he absolutely will toss me onto the bed if I don't do what he said.

So I crawl across it on all fours, glancing over my shoulder at him while I move. And yeah, I'm teasing him with my smile and my body. Getting Nick hot and bothered is my favorite sport.

I lie down on my stomach with a pillow under my head and my cheek resting on it. "I'm ready for my surprise. Please tell me it involves multiple orgasms."

"If I do it right, it will." He climbs onto the bed, kneeling at my feet. "Just relax and enjoy this. Fair warning, though. I will need to fuck you hard when I finish with your surprise."

"You damn well better."

He sets a hand on the mattress alongside my shoulder, bending over me. Then he slides his other hand into my hair and begins to massage my scalp with his fingertips, moving them in easy, seductive circles.

I start to squirm. The way he touches me always makes me desperate to have him inside me, but tonight it's different, the need more intense. Who knew a scalp massage could make me feel this way?

Nick settles his palm on my scalp too and rubs it slowly while he keeps moving his fingertips.

A moan escapes my lips, vibrating in my throat.

He picks up a glass bottle and twists the cap off, then pours a measure of oil onto his palm. While he gently rubs his palms together, he keeps his gaze riveted to my face.

"What is that?" I ask.

"Massage oil." He leans in to murmur, "Vanilla flavored. I'm warming it up for you."

"Flavored?"

"It's edible massage oil. I'm going to rub this all over you, then lick it off."

My pulse quickens, and my skin tightens, like my body can't wait for Nick Hunter to fondle me from head to toe. *I* can't wait. The anticipation alone is driving me crazy in the best way.

He straddles my legs and lays his big, slick palms on my back, dragging them down my body inch by inch while the scent of vanilla mingles with the sandalwood and ginger from the candles. I inhale a deep breath so I can let the aromas fill my senses as he glides his hands ever lower, skimming them over my bottom and down my thighs.

"You have the most beautiful body I've ever seen, Siobhan." He smooths his palms down my calves until he reaches my feet, then he begins to knead my soles. "Your skin feels like silk, and the scent of your cream intoxicates me better than any alcohol. I could massage your body all night long and never get enough."

The way his fingers work my feet… That's intoxicating me. I can't help exhaling a long, throaty moan.

He sweeps his hands up my body, resting them on my shoulders. "Time to rub you down, then lick you clean."

"Oh yes, please."

Nick walks his fingers up my neck and begins to massage my nape with his fingertips. He works his way down to my shoulders, where he kneads the muscles with his strong fingers so expertly that I feel myself relaxing even while I'm getting more and more turned on. I'm so wet I can feel the evidence of my lust between my thighs, dribbling down my skin. He uses his thumbs and knuckles to knead a path down my back while his cock brushes my skin. When he reaches my ass, he lays a palm on each cheek and rubs with his fingers until I'm so aroused that I'm clutching the pillow and struggling to catch my breath.

His lips curve into the naughtiest smile I've ever seen, and he plants both hands on the mattress at either side of my shoulders. His lips part. His tongue slides out. He hesitates like that, his eyes half-closed, for so long that I'm about to kick him. But then he lowers his head and starts to lick a trail down my spine.

I clench my fingers in the pillow even harder, squeezing my eyes shut. The sensation of his warm, velvety tongue on my skin makes me more excited than I ever knew I could be. Somehow, his erotic massage is relaxing and exciting at the same time. He keeps licking until he reaches my ass, then he slowly sinks his teeth into one cheek.

When he swirls his tongue over my skin, I moan again, even louder than before.

He slaps my ass. "Roll over."

Though he's still straddling me, I find I can roll over. Now I have the full view of Nick's body towering over me, his cock suspended between us with the tip red and glistening. I lick my lips as I remember what it was like to take that beauty in my mouth. "You're the sexiest man in the world, Nick. I've been with other men, but with you, I feel like I'm a virgin again."

"Yes, I am *that* good." His smirk assures me he's joking.

But he really is *that* good.

Nick gets more oil and warms it in his palms, then he spreads it over my chest and massages my breasts, flicking his thumbs over the tips of my nipples.

I'm gasping for breath while my heart thrashes in my chest. "Please, Nick, I can't take it anymore. I need—Oh God, I need—"

"Take a moment to breathe." He sits back on his heels. "Slow and easy, pet. In and out, in and out."

I follow his instructions, and little by little, the almost painful need to come softens until I no longer feel wildly desperate for a climax. How does he do that? Nick always knows what I need and how to give it to me.

He brushes the backs of his fingers across my cheek, the scent of vanilla teasing my senses. "Ready for the most erotic part of this massage?"

"Yes."

"If it's too much, tell me. I can skip straight to making you come."

"No, I want it all. Please, Nick."

He pushes one knee between my thighs. "Spread your legs for me."

I can't resist anything he wants me to do, and besides, I essentially begged him to do this. So I spread my legs.

Nick kneels between my feet, lowers himself until he's held up by one hand on the bed, and aims those baby blues right at me. For a moment, we just look at each other. I swear I feel erotic energy sizzling between us—or maybe that's my sex burning for him. His erection dangles between our bodies, and a single drop of moisture falls off it to land on my belly.

He rocks his hips forward to glide his length into me all the way, only to pull out and thrust into me again. A look of intense concentration tightens his features as he pulls out and grasps his cock with one hand, rocking forward to push the head of his erection into my clitoris.

A jolt of pleasure explodes inside me. I fist my hands in the pillow so hard my fingers ache and let out a sharp, desperate sound.

He bumps his cock into my clit again and again in rhythmic movements that shoot pleasure through me from my aching nub straight into my sex. My breaths become gasps that burst out of me in time with his movements.

Suddenly, he swipes his dick down my cleft, then rubs it side to side as he drags it back up. His head collides with my clit, but he doesn't stop there. He scrapes his crown along my cleft again and slides it back up in that zigzagging motion until he bumps into my nub. He keeps doing that, over and over until I'm thrashing and gasping and pounding my fists on the mattress.

He pulls away, only for a second, then rubs his cock up and down the length of my cleft in swift but measured strokes.

My entire body freezes up, my mouth falls open, and I can't breathe anymore. My ears start to ring, but just when I think I'll pass out from how incredible this feels, an orgasm rocks me from head to toe. My legs fold up, my back flattens into the mattress, and my head snaps forward as a cry is wrenched from my throat. My inner muscles clench at nothing, but I keep coming until I can't take it any longer.

I collapse, breathing so hard I can't speak.

Nick is breathing hard too. His face is cinched up in the most erotic expression of unquenched lust that I've ever seen. He's never looked hotter.

He swipes a hand up his face, into his hair. "Need to—I can't—Now."

I love that he wants me so much he can't form complete sentences, but I can't stand for him to wait one second longer. "Do it, Nick, now. Take me any way you need to."

Chapter Twenty-Three

Gazing down at Siobhan, at her naked and oil-slicked body, I can't remember any of the things I wanted to do with her tonight. All my brain can do is command me to fuck her. Or maybe that's my dick telling me that. Either way, I need to do it. But I can't seem to move a muscle, not even to blink, so my eyes are burning and my cock is throbbing.

"Is something wrong?" she asks.

Since I doubt I can manage to do anything except grunt, I shake my head to let her know there's nothing wrong with me. Sure, I'm paralyzed. But I'm not having a stroke. I just can't believe what I've done with Siobhan. An erotic massage? I swore I'd never give any woman the sort of "special" massage Georgina Prescott told everyone I offer—for a fee. But doing this for Siobhan isn't about money, or even about my skills as a massage therapist. It's about her. This is all for her.

The woman beneath me rises to her knees and crawls closer. She skates her palms up and down my chest. "I think you need a minute, hmm? Lie down and let me relax you."

"I can't—That—"

She lays two fingers on my lips. "Hush, Nick. Don't you trust me?"

Nodding is the only response I can give her.

"Then lie down on your back." She moves to the side, waving toward the mattress. "Let me give you something special too."

Since I seem to have gone mute, I see no point in kneeling here like a moron. I lie down on the bed. If she means to give me a "special" massage, I might just have a stroke after all. But as I gaze up at her, drinking in every curve and swell on her glistening body, I know I want her to do that to me. I don't care if she makes me come so hard I die of a heart attack. I'll be the happiest bloke in heaven.

Never in my life have I delayed my own orgasm to make a woman happy. With Siobhan, I don't want to rush any part of this. Even if she kills me in the process.

She grabs the bottle and rubs some of the vanilla oil onto her palms.

Fuck, just watching her do that has me fighting the intense urge to fist my hand around my cock and finish myself off. When her hands settle on my shoulders, I suck in a ragged breath. She rubs her palms all over my chest until the oil shimmers on my skin, then she kneads my muscles with her thumbs. I want to flip us over and slam into her, but I also don't want to do that. She's so beautiful, with her hair falling around her face and the oil giving her skin a sensual sheen. Instead of grasping her, I grip the headboard.

She bends toward me and drags her tongue up from my hips to my collarbone.

A deep groan vibrates in my chest. Finally, I drum up a few words. "This—isn't—relaxing me."

"No?" She shimmies forward to straddle my hips. "Well, I can't let you suffer."

Siobhan rises onto her knees.

I have an idea of what she means to do, so I nod toward the bedside table. "Condom."

She gets a condom packet out of the drawer and kneels over me again.

I reach for the packet.

"Uh-uh-uh, Nick." She runs the packet's edge across her lips. "I'm in charge now, so shut up and take it."

She knows I love it when she's bossy. So I lie back and let her do whatever she wants.

Ripping open the condom packet with her teeth, she tosses it away and rolls the latex over me inch by inch, going so slowly that

I lose my breath and grip the headboard again. By the time she's covered me, I'm halfway to coming. I open my mouth to tell her that, but I don't get the chance.

She impales her body on my cock and fucks me. I can't do anything except watch her rise up and slam back down onto me, her breasts bouncing and her eyes half-closed. I grasp her hips and urge her to rock them, needing to penetrate her even more deeply. Her wetness trickles down her inner thighs and my cock, the scent of it mingling with the aromas of vanilla, ginger, and sandalwood. I'd never thought of smells as erotic, but tonight, I do.

Because of her.

She rolls her hips, then pushes up until only the head of my cock is inside her, and plunges down again. Over and over, she does that, until we're both gasping and damp with sweat and I can't take it anymore.

I flip us over and seize her hips to thrust into her so hard and fast the bed thumps into the wall in time with my thrusts and she starts writhing, her mouth open as wild cries erupt out of her. I feel her muscles tightening around me, and I know she's about to climax. Holding back for even one more second takes all the willpower I have and then some, but I stop myself from coming for just long enough, until her body pulsates around me.

Then I let go.

A sensation, like fire and electricity, barrels through me, and my body bows inward. I come while her muscles are still clenching me, come so hard I think I might've gone blind for a split second there even while I keep thrusting. Noises echo in the room, but I can't tell if I'm shouting or she is. Maybe we both are. By the time I'm done, I can't move, frozen with my hands clamped around her hips.

She seems dazed, so at least I'm not the only one who can't think.

Finally, I fall onto the bed beside her.

"Holy shit, Nick." She laughs, but it's breathless because we're both still gasping. "You absolutely are *that* good."

I try to chuckle but can't quite pull it off. "So are you, Siobhan."

We lie here for a few minutes without speaking, until we can breathe normally again. Then she rolls over to lie half on top of me. "That massage was incredible. Your girlfriends must've loved dating you."

"Why would you say that?"

"Because you give mind-blowing dirty massages."

"I've never done that for anyone else."

She pushes up on one elbow to look at me. "What? But you're so good at it."

"Thank you, but I never wanted to do it for anyone else. Only for you. Wasn't sure I should, though."

"Why not?"

I rub my eyes, strictly to avoid looking at her. "I've wanted to give you that sort of massage since the day we met, but I worried if I did, that might convince you I'm exactly what Georgina Prescott has everyone believing I am."

"You are not a gigolo, Nick. Not a pimp or a brothel-keeper either." She pries my fingers away from my eyes. "I never thought you were. I did suspect you're an insatiable man who would strain my willpower to its limits, but I didn't mind that."

"And I suspected you'd be a fantastic lover once you gave up being so uptight."

She taps my chest with one finger. "Ha-ha. I wasn't uptight. I was…dedicated to maintaining my integrity as a teacher."

"Why did you give up your ethics to be with me? If anyone finds out we're sleeping together, you could be sacked."

"I have tenure, so that makes it harder for the university to fire me. They could still do it, but I don't care. My job isn't as reward-ing as it used to be." She sits up and stretches her arms above her head. "I've learned there are things that matter more than work or status."

I want to ask her a question, but I don't know if she'll take it the wrong way. Better wait a bit longer before I ask whether I'm the reason she feels differently about her work these days.

Siobhan sweeps her gaze around the room. "If you've never given an erotic massage before, how did you have all the stuff on hand? You know, the oil and candles."

"I've had the candles for ages. Women love a romantic atmo-sphere during sex." I sit up too, but instead of stretching, I scratch the back of my neck. "I, uh, bought the oil just for you. Took me two weeks to work up the nerve to offer you a massage."

"Just for me? Nick, that's…so incredibly sweet."

"You deserved something special."

She drapes an arm across my shoulders. "I've been meaning to ask. What was that amazing thing you did at the end of my massage? Nobody's ever tried that before."

"It's called kunyaza. The technique was traditionally practiced in Central Africa, but I learned it from an Algerian masseuse. We met at a conference and hit it off, so she taught me her favorite sexual technique."

"Uh-huh." Siobhan's smile is almost a smirk. "And by 'hit it off,' you mean you slept with her."

"Well, yes. I was single, you know."

"I'm not criticizing. Maybe I should send that masseuse a thank-you note for teaching you how to make me come so hard I think I left my body for a couple seconds." She kisses my cheek. "You're the first non-asshole boyfriend I've ever had."

"Not sure if I should be grateful for that comment. I'm not an arsehole? That doesn't mean I'm—"

"You're an incredible boyfriend, Nick, in every way. An amazing man, period."

"And you're an incredible woman." We're gazing into each other's eyes, and suddenly, I can't stop myself from saying something I shouldn't. "I love you, Siobhan."

She opens her mouth, about to speak.

My mobile rings.

"Bollocks," I hiss. "Hold that thought."

I leap off the bed and find my trousers, then dig my mobile out of a pocket. The screen tells me it's Richard ringing me. I swipe to take the call. "What is it, Rick? I'm naked in bed with my girlfriend."

The fact that I'm standing up, not lying in bed, has no bearing on what I said. I'm still naked, after all.

Siobhan smiles, and I can tell she's laughing quietly because her shoulders shake.

"I'm sorry for disturbing your urgent business," Rick says, "but I've been tasked with informing you."

"Of what?" I'm getting a knot in my gut just hearing him say the word informing.

"The American Wives Club have a surprise for you. They've worked bloody hard to set this up, so don't get shirty about it."

"Why aren't you on your honeymoon yet?"

"Maddie wanted to stay to see your face when you receive the surprise. She was instrumental in making this happen." He switches to his big-brother voice. Richard might be only two minutes and thirty-eight seconds older than I am, but he still thinks he's my big brother. "Don't get shirty, Nick."

"Stop saying that, would you? I'm a mature businessman, just like you." I switch to my snarky, slightly younger brother voice. "Though I am a lot more fun than you. Should I get Siobhan on the phone to confirm that?"

The woman herself falls back onto the bed and laughs audibly.

I cup my hand over the phone's speaker. "You're not behaving like a good girlfriend right now. I might need to take back what I said about you."

She makes a zipper motion across her mouth, but her shoulders are shaking again.

"All right, Rick," I tell my brother. "Since I'm sure I have no choice, I'll meet you lot wherever this surprise is going to happen. I'm sure it'll be the dog's bollocks."

Yes, I'm being sarcastic about the last part. I don't honestly think I'll enjoy whatever those women have planned for me.

"Meet us in front of your spa at noon. Goodbye, Nick."

Richard hangs up before I can demand to know what the bloody hell is going to happen at noon. In front of my spa. Because of the American Wives Club.

My mobile rings again.

"What is it now, Rick?" I ask when I take the call.

"Change of plans. Mum and Dad insist you and Siobhan come to brunch at their house. Be there at ten."

"All right, fine. See you at ten." I end the call and toss my mobile onto the bedside table. "We're having brunch at my parents' house."

"That sounds like fun. And it'll give you a chance to talk to your family."

"I talk to them all the time."

"Not about your feelings." She slides off the bed and clasps my hands. "They need to know the real reason you quit school and the real reason this idiotic rumor upsets you."

"I haven't spent nineteen years feeling like a useless wanker. Never regretted leaving university either. So there's no need for me to—"

"Yes, Nick, there is a need. Clear the air. Get the truth out there." She leans into me, tipping her head back to meet my gaze. "You know what they say. The truth shall set you free."

"I've been free all along."

"You've led a happy and fulfilling life, but you still need to tell your family what really happened. Then, this rumor won't have any sway over you anymore."

She's right. I know that, but I've never been good at explaining my feelings. It's easier to tell Siobhan about these things because…I love her. I don't know if she loves me. After I said those words, she seemed like she was about to speak.

Until my mobile rang.

"I'll be there with you," she says. "For moral support."

"Not moral support and sex? I might need a good shag after my confession."

"Whatever you need, I'm here to give it."

Is it any wonder why I fell in love with her?

But now it's time to lay down on that guillotine and accept my fate.

Chapter Twenty-Four

Siobhan

With everything that's gone on lately, with that rumor and now the American Wives Club's surprise, I thought it would be much harder to convince Nick to tell his family why he quit college. He agreed without even getting snarky about it. We arrive at his parents' house at ten o'clock to enjoy a lovely brunch with the Hunters. Richard and Maddie haven't left for the Caribbean yet, and though they had planned to go straight from their London hotel to the airport, they insisted on coming home for brunch when Pippa called them.

They also stayed for the big surprise. Maddie helped arrange it, but she won't tell me what's involved.

"Just promise me it won't embarrass Nick," I say to her. "He's sensitive about…stuff lately."

"Don't worry," Maddie assures me. "Nick might blush a little, but he'll like it. We're doing this to help him, after all, not to make him feel worse. We love Nick to pieces."

Nick Hunter is the most amazing man I've ever met, but I don't know if I love him yet. He spoke those words to me—"I love you, Siobhan"—but I didn't get the chance to respond. Just as well. I have no idea how to respond. In the month we've known each other, he's come to mean more to me than anyone in the world except for my daughter. Felicity thinks Nick is "awesome" and "the first non-douchebag" I've ever dated. Yeah, I politely scolded her for using that word. I'm still her mother, even if she is eighteen and living on her own now.

Felicity has also made sly suggestions that I should marry Nick. Luckily, she never said that in front of him. But considering his declaration of love, I guess he wouldn't mind if someone suggested we might tie the knot.

I tried that once, and it ended in misery.

Nick is different, though. He's funny, sexy, sweet, and smart. He owns his own business and loves his family. I've never been attracted to a man at first sight, but with him, I was ready to have sex thirty seconds after he walked into my office. Well, it might've been closer to ten seconds. Or maybe three.

Okay, I lusted for him at first sight.

"You and Nick are so good together," Maddie says.

"How do you know that?" I ask.

"Anyone can see it." Maddie and I are sitting on lawn chairs while Nick talks to his brother and his parents on the patio. She leans over to touch my arm. "I haven't known Nick that long, but Richard says his brother has never looked at any woman the way he looks at you."

"We've only been dating for a month."

"I knew I loved Rick after less than two weeks." She sighs, her expression turning softer and almost sentimental. "Honestly, though, I think I knew the moment I met him. Never used to believe in love at first sight. My sister teased me about it back when I was still getting to know Rick, but it took me a while to accept that I did fall for him right away."

"Math is my thing. I need an equation that makes sense, and love at first sight doesn't fit into any of the mathematical models I know."

"But there is pi. It's an irrational number."

I freeze. Not that long ago, Nick had asked me about pi, and I explained how it's an irrational number that has no end and never repeats itself. Now Maddie mentions pi. Is this some kind of sign? If so, I have no idea what the universe is trying to tell me. Maddie is a scientist, so it's not strange for her to know about pi.

But still…

Love at first sight? I can't believe in that because of a math problem.

Maddie gives me a knowing smile. "Just keep an open mind, that's all I'm saying."

"I always try to do that, but sometimes I fail."

Brunch hasn't been served yet because Nick wanted to explain things to his family first. I'm guessing he was too anxious to eat.

The Hunters have an adorable cottage, and I can't help wondering what it would be like to live in a village like this one. Cockshire is cute and homey despite the rumor garbage. Can't blame an entire town for that.

But I do blame that woman, Lady Georgina Prescott, for the whole debacle and the emotional damage it's wrought on my boyfriend. How can anyone defame a hard-working, amazing man like Nick? He would never do anything to hurt anyone. Look at how patient he's been with me. I was kind of rude when we first met, which I now realize was my subconscious way of covering up the fact I was attracted to him, but Nick treated me with nothing but kindness.

Well, flirtation and kindness.

If that scandal had never happened, I would never have met him. So maybe good can come out of a bad thing.

That's still no excuse for what Georgina Prescott did to Nick.

I've never felt vengeful before, but when it comes to Nick and Georgina, I want to exact some serious vengeance on her ass. Does that mean something? I don't know. Maybe it means I have deeper feelings for him than I've wanted to admit.

My gaze wanders to where Nick and his family are sitting around a patio table chatting. He looks anxious.

"Think I'll go over," I tell Maddie. "To give Nick moral support."

"You go help your honey," she says. "You two are the cutest couple."

"Uh, thank you." I start to walk away, then hesitate, glancing at Maddie. "Maybe you should come too. You're part of the family, after all, and what Nick needs to say involves your husband."

"Let's go support our guys together."

We stroll over to the patio, but there aren't any chairs available. So Maddie sits on Richard's lap, and I sit on Nick's.

He raises his brows at me.

I whisper in his ear, "Moral support."

"Rick needs that too?" he says in an equally soft voice while rolling his eyes toward his brother.

"Did you tell them yet?"

He flattens his lips and twists them this way and that.

I take that as a no. "Go on, get it over with. Everything will be okay."

Pippa Hunter smiles at us. "Are you two talking about when to get married?"

She's joking. I think.

"No," I tell Nick's mom. "Not yet."

Why did I say "not yet"? Pippa will think I'm in love with her son. Maybe I am. Comforting him during his big confession matters a lot to me, and I never want to see Nick humiliated or hurt.

While I gaze into his beautiful eyes, the truth hits me so hard I almost gasp. Oh God, I do love him.

"Let's eat first," Nick says to everyone.

"No procrastinating," I tell him, loud enough for everyone to hear.

"You're right, I know." Nick clears his throat. "I have something to tell all of you. So, here goes."

Chapter Twenty-Five

Nick

I tell them everything—why I quit school, why that rumor upset me so much, and why I ran away to America because of it. They're going to think I'm an idiot, aren't they? I deserve their scorn, but I know they won't give me any of that. I've also assured them I have not been feeling like a failure for all these years or worrying women like Rick better than they like me. It's only been over the past two months that I've felt that way again.

Yes, it's all Lady Prescott's fault.

But I should thank Georgina for being a spiteful cow, I suppose, since I wouldn't have met Siobhan otherwise.

No, I'll thank fate for that, not Lady Sodding Prescott.

My parents and my brother are looking at me like they want to laugh.

Luckily, Siobhan is still seated on my lap. Her bum on my thighs makes me feel much better about being a complete moron.

"That's what you think?" Richard says. "Dad gave me the company because he doesn't trust you to run it properly. And I stole your girlfriend. Gina? I barely even remember that silly bint. I only sh—uh, went out with her once, then she took up with a footballer, the star player on the uni team."

He almost said he'd shagged her, which I already knew, but he seems to think that revelation will shock our parents. Or maybe he doesn't want Maddie to know about that.

But it's what he did say that surprises me.

"Gina did what?" I say. "How did I never know that?"

"Because we weren't, ah, seeing much of each other back then."

Yes, my polite brother is trying not to offend me, though I can't see why he'd think the fact we weren't best mates back then would bother me.

Well… All right, maybe it did bother me a little. At the time. Not now, though. Rick and I are close these days, so the past doesn't matter.

Our father smiles and shakes his head. "Do you think Mother and I don't know what you two are talking about? Nick enjoyed a bit of 'how's your father' with a silly chit who then threw him over for Rick, and he enjoyed the same favor until the girl threw him over too. For heaven's sake, Pippa and I aren't prudes, you know. We realize our adult sons have sex from time to time. Do you think Mother and I don't?"

Honestly, I prefer not to dwell on what my parents get up to in private. Yes, I'm a forty-year-old man who doesn't want to know that his parents shag. That's hardly the most idiotic thing I've ever done.

My mother shakes her head at me. "Nicholas Timothy Hunter, you ruddy fool. We know you didn't give up on university because your girlfriend got a leg over with Rick. You did it because you were never that keen on school. You're a clever boy, but some people just aren't meant for the academic life."

"You're spot on, Pippa," my father says. "But Nick insisted he wanted to go to university, so we let him do it."

I groan. "Yes, I know I'm not as clever as Rick."

"That's bollocks," my brother announces loudly. "Nick, you got high marks in all your classes. Your academic record was better than mine."

"No, you're only trying to make me feel better. It's all right. I haven't spent my entire life feeling worthless, not because of you and not because I dropped out of uni. So there's no need to bolster my ego."

Mum gives me a stern, motherly look. "Nicholas Timothy Hunter, you listen to me. You did better at school than your brother. Do you think I'd lie about that?"

Of course she wouldn't. Mum is always honest with us. Besides, the fact she called me by my full name twice means she is serious about this.

I got better marks than Richard. Blimey.

Dad is giving me a stern, fatherly look. "For the record, we don't think less of you because you never finished your degree. How many people can start a business from scratch and not only make a go of it, but turn it into a successful venture? You've run your day spa for more than a decade, and it's still going strong. We're very proud of you, Nick."

My throat has gotten tight, and my eyes feel… No, I'm not getting choked up because my father said he's proud of me. That would be stupid.

But my eyes have gotten watery.

Siobhan folds her arms around my neck and kisses my cheek. Then she whispers to me, "It's okay to get emotional in front of your family. I'll still want to get naked with you later. Nothing in the world could make me not want to be with you, with or without clothes."

Maybe I was wondering if she'd want me less after this. But only a little. And not anymore.

I slip my arms around Siobhan and speak to everyone. "It's that rumor Georgina Prescott started that made me feel…uncertain. If everyone is willing to believe I'd prostitute myself or turn my business into a brothel, then they'd believe almost anything. But spending some time in America has helped me see that it doesn't matter what anyone says. I'm proud of the business I built and the life I've made for myself."

"You should be proud, Nick," Richard says. "We're all bloody proud of you, for sure."

"Of course we are," Dad says. "Couldn't be prouder, son."

Mum leaps up to plant a kiss on my cheek. "I'm the luckiest woman on earth to have two sons who have made me so proud."

I roll my eyes. "If you lot say the word proud again, it'll start to sound like gibberish."

But yes, I'm only being snarky to hide the fact I'm getting a bit choked up again.

Maddie whispers something to Rick, and he nods. They both stand up.

Rick clears his throat. "It's time for Nick's surprise. The American Wives Club are waiting for us in Cockshire."

We all climb into my parents' car and travel to the town that has been my home for more than a decade. Rick drove, and he parks the car a full block away from the spa and on a side street that has no view of the building.

"Why did you park here?" I ask my brother as we get out of the car. "There must be spots available on the other street."

He claps a hand on my shoulder. "You need the exercise, mate."

Right. Because I look like an overweight couch potato, don't I?

I imagine our side approach to the spa is part of the surprise those nosy American women have cooked up for me.

After I've helped Siobhan out of the car, Rick hands me a handkerchief. "Fold this up and tie it over your eyes."

"It's pink. Afraid that color doesn't suit my complexion. Now, if you've got a mauve one…"

"Just do what I said, you cheeky arse."

"This handkerchief must belong to the lovely Madeleine," I say as I fold up the fabric. "Unless you have a softer side I've never seen before, Rick."

"Don't make me regret helping the women arrange this for you."

"It's mine," Maddie says. "Rick looks best in blue. So do you, Nick. You're twins, after all, which means you have the same complexion."

"No mauve, then? I'm heartbroken." I tie the blindfold around my head. "There, I'm ready. But how am I meant to walk like this?"

"Siobhan will help you," Richard says. "Won't you?"

"Absolutely." She slips her arm around mine. "Do you trust me to guide you?"

"I trust you to do anything for me."

Siobhan leads me away, and I can hear other footfalls ahead of and behind us, which tells me everyone is coming along on this mystery visit to the spa. The beautiful woman on my arm informs me when we reach the corner, so I won't trip over the curb and fall flat on my arse. We need to walk slowly to accommodate my temporary blindness, but we arrive at our destination a few minutes later.

"What now?" Siobhan asks.

"No bloody idea," I say.

"I was talking to your brother."

She keeps her arm hooked around mine even as two man-size hands rotate me to the left.

"Now he's in position," Rick says. Then he moves away and shouts, "Ladies, you're up."

"Take the blindfold off," a woman calls out. That sounds like Rika.

"I'll do that," Siobhan says, and then she whips the blindfold off.

My eyes had gotten used to the semi-darkness, and I squint at the bright sunlight that's now shining in my face. I need a few seconds to understand what I'm seeing.

We stand in front of the spa entrance, facing toward the street, a few feet from the curb. In the street, I see a crowd of ladies in front and men in the back, lined up like they're soldiers guarding their women.

Emery MacTaggart, wife of Rory the Steely Solicitor, steps away from the group to stand inches from the curb. "This is your surprise, Nick. What do you think?"

"Well, it's very nice to see you girls, but…" I look at the crowd and notice many more familiar faces there. "What are you lot doing here? I'm not getting shirty, just confused."

She smiles and spreads her arms wide. "The American Wives Club has organized this event to show our love and support for you, Nick. And we're not alone."

Emery glances over her shoulder and nods once.

One of the gents in the back—Logan MacTaggart, it looks like—blows a whistle.

People pour out of the side streets and shops, filling the roadway and the pavements along both sides. Soon, my family and I are surrounded by more than the American women and their spouses, but also by a large group of strangers. I see my employees too, including Bennett Montague.

A young man carrying a large camera squeezes through the crowd. "May I take a few pictures, Mr. Hunter?"

"Which Mr. Hunter are you asking?"

"Sorry. I meant you, Nick Hunter."

"Uh, sure, go on." I glance around and ask anyone who cares to answer, "What is going on here?"

"This is your redemption," Maddie says. "The cute young guy behind you works for the Cockshire newspaper. He's going to document this gathering so everyone will know how much the people of this town appreciate and believe in you. Chance and Rory have also filed a libel suit against Lady Prescott on your behalf. Once we're done, nobody will ever claim you do anything at your spa other than give the best massages in Essex. Legitimate massages."

Can their show of support actually redeem my business and my reputation? Maybe it was never as damaged as I'd assumed. That meme rubbish on social media had convinced me everyone must think I run a brothel. But the people of Cockshire, the town I've called home for years, have turned out en masse to prove me wrong.

Even if some people still believe what Georgina said, I don't care anymore. My family, my mates, and the woman I love have always stood by me.

And now, an entire town does too.

"We love Nick!" Emery shouts, pumping her fist in the air. "We love Nick! We love Nick!"

Soon, more voices join her chant. At first, it's the American Wives Club screaming my name. Then, their husbands join in, and soon, it seems like everyone in the whole town is chanting their fervent support for me.

My eyes have grown watery, and a few tears roll down my cheeks. It's embarrassing, but I can't help it. I wipe my eyes and turn to the woman beside me.

Siobhan lifts onto her tiptoes and cradles my face in her hands, leaning in until her lips almost touch mine. "I love you, Nick."

Then she kisses me.

And I forget all about the crowd.

Chapter Twenty-Six

We fly back to America a few hours later, but only after the mayor of Cockshire makes an announcement. He tells the entire town that Nick Hunter is a valued, honorable member of the community who has provided a much-needed service to the town. Nick's Nirvana has helped countless people who have injuries and those who simply need the stress relief that a good massage can provide.

I was surprised when Nick cried a little, but he does it again after the mayor's speech. If he thinks a few tears make him any less hot, I'll prove him wrong during the flight home.

And I do. Twice.

Felicity meets us at Nick's apartment. Though we're tired from the journey, jet lag, and the emotional conclusion to our visit with his family, we both want to tell Felicity all about it before we crash. When we get to the end, the part where an entire town demonstrated their support for Nick, she starts to cry and hugs him hard.

"What was that for?" he asks when she finally lets go.

"You rock, and finally, everyone knows that. You'll be an awesome stepdad."

"Stepdad?"

I intervene before my daughter can shock my boyfriend any worse. "Let's order pizza. I'm starving."

"Can we get dessert pizza too?" Felicity asks.

"Sure. Let's order breadsticks and make it a real pig-out."

Once Felicity leaves, we get naked and collapse onto the bed together, falling asleep right away. With the time difference, we gained seven hours from our journey home, so we manage to sleep for twelve hours but still wake up on time.

For a week, we go back to our normal lives. Nick goes to class, I go to work, and every night we have dinner together in his apartment or mine. I finally decided I don't care if anyone sees me with Nick. We're forty-something adults, not a sleazy older professor and her innocent young student. I haven't taken advantage of Nick. If I get fired for being with him, I don't care.

For the first time in ages, the thought of losing my job doesn't scare me, and my work matters less than my personal life. I always made Felicity my priority, giving up opportunities to go to faculty parties and brownnose. Now, though, I have two people who matter more than my career.

I know Nick misses his family, and he worries about his business. Sure, he's got Bennett and his other employees to handle things. Ben is such a sweetheart, and according to Nick, amazing at his job. I wonder if the American Wives Club will help him find his true love. I still don't know the secret Ben said he'd tell me later, but my curiosity can wait.

I miss Nick's family too. They're such wonderful people.

A week after we came home, Nick and I are snuggling on the sofa in my apartment when the phone rings. I answer it without glancing at the caller ID.

"Dr. Griffin, we have a problem."

I recognize the voice of the dean of the math department. "What is it? If another student cheated—"

"No, that's not the issue." He pauses for a couple of seconds. "Have you been dating a student?"

Oh shit. I'd known this might happen sometime, but I hadn't expected it so soon.

I won't lie, so I tell the dean, "Yes, I'm involved with Nick Hunter."

"Dr. Griffin, why?" he says with a sigh, clearly disappointed in me. "You were seen together, by a group of students and a faculty member. They said you two were holding hands and kissing. I have no choice but to report this to the ethics committee."

"I know. It's okay, do what you need to do."

We say goodbye, and I turn to Nick. He's still sitting beside me, though he now wears a concerned look.

"Is something wrong?" he asks.

"Yeah. That was the dean. Somebody saw us together looking lovey-dovey, and he has no choice but to report me to the ethics committee."

"This is my fault. I shouldn't have pursued you and—"

"No, Nick, this is not your fault. I kissed you first, and I ripped your shirt open and begged you to screw me. Besides, things might not be as bad as they seem."

"I don't want to be responsible for you losing your job."

"Let's not panic right off the bat. We should wait and see what happens."

"All right. We'll wait."

That night, we sleep together—just sleep. Nick holds me in his arms until morning, then we get up and get back to living our lives. Whatever the ethics committee decides, I know our relationship will survive it.

A few days later, I'm called into the dean's office. It's judgment day.

The meeting doesn't go as badly as I'd expected.

I'm in my office—sitting at my desk staring, at the lesson plans I'd crafted yesterday—when Nick strides through the door.

He halts in front of my desk, looking more serious than I've ever seen him before. "What did they do to you?"

"Nothing much. They decided what I did wasn't grounds for dismissal, though I will be on administrative leave for the rest of the summer session. What about you?"

"I've been expelled."

A wave of cold floods through me. "Expelled? They can't do that. Why would they punish you more harshly than me?"

"You have a long history of being a valuable member of the faculty who has a spotless record. I'm a new student who's been the object of a nasty rumor. Of course they'd keep you, and I'm glad they did." He sighs and rubs his jaw, and I notice the dark circles under his eyes. "My student visa has been revoked, which means I have to go home."

"What?" I spring out of my chair. "We'll fight this. You will get to finish your degree."

"No, I won't."

"Then I'm going with you."

He comes around the desk to take my hands in his. "You have a life here, Siobhan. Don't make a rash decision because I have to leave. Take your time. Think about what you really want and then decide."

I know what I want, but he doesn't give me the chance to say it.

Nick Hunter walks out of my office and out of my life.

Oh, like hell he will.

Chapter Twenty-Seven

Nick

Yesterday, I walked away from the only woman I've ever loved. Am I a complete idiot? Clearly, the answer is yes. I told her to take her time and think about things, about us. She wanted to come home with me, but I couldn't let her do that on the spur of the moment. Siobhan needs to consider all the ramifications before she commits to moving to another country for me.

But I wanted to beg her to do that. Right away, not in…however long it might take for her to think about it.

I arrived home late yesterday, UK time, and my family and friends immediately announced that I need to be cheered up. They've organized a backyard party at my house in Cockshire. Since I've never paid much attention to my backyard, all the barmy people who love me brought everything we need for this party—outdoor furniture, a barbecue grill, and of course, beer.

My brother has made it his mission to ensure I enjoy myself this afternoon. He's awful at that, but I appreciate the effort.

Rick insists on sitting beside me at one of the small tables that have been set up in my yard. And he insists on telling me, repeatedly, that I should fly back to America and "retrieve" Siobhan.

"She's not a piece of lost luggage," I say. "Besides, my visa was revoked. I can't go anywhere near America."

"You lost your student visa. Get one for travel."

"I'm probably on the no-fly list. Can't let randy British massage therapists defile those American girls."

"Nick, you—" Rick stares at something past my shoulder. Just when I'm going to smack him, strictly to make sure he hasn't gone comatose, he returns his attention to me and grins. "Turn around, Nick."

"Why?"

"Do it, you bloody moron."

I twist around in my chair to glance behind me. There, on the other side of the yard, Siobhan is speaking to Maddie. Then she notices me, smiles, and starts walking this way.

For a moment, I can't believe what I'm seeing—until my brother kicks me in the shin.

"Wake up, you lucky sod," he says. "Go and get her."

I don't need to "get her." By the time I stand up, Siobhan has reached me.

She grabs my shirt and pulls me close, clucking her tongue. "Nicholas Timothy Hunter, did you really think you could walk out like that and I wouldn't chase after you?"

"Not sure. I thought you'd be taking time to think."

"Did all the thinking I need to do." She boosts up on her tiptoes, her lips millimeters from mine. "I quit my job."

"Why?"

"Partly because I'm tired of working my ass off and not having any fun." She presses her chest to mine, crushing those tits I adore into my body. "But mostly, I did it for you."

I'm starting to feel lightheaded, probably because I've stopped breathing and my heart is pounding. "What about Felicity and your parents?"

"Felicity is a grown woman. She doesn't need me anymore." Siobhan gets a sly look on her face. "Besides, I heard a rumor you have several friends who own private jets. My parents and my daughter can visit us anytime."

No, it's not a rumor. I'm done with that rot. But I love that she's teasing me.

I lay my hands over hers on my chest. "If you're sure…"

"Positive. I love you, Nick Hunter, and the only place where I belong is with you."

"Well, in that case…" I drop to one knee and clasp her hand. "Will you marry me, Siobhan?"

"Yes, I'd love to."

My friends and family—*our* friends and family—clap, cheer, and whistle.

I pull out the little surprise I have for her and flip open the ring box. "Bought this three days after we got home from England."

Siobhan holds out her hand. "You never waste time, do you?"

"No." I slip the ring onto her finger and stand. "I'm more the rush-in-headlong sort."

"Turns out I am too." She kisses me. "But only with you."

"I hope you don't mind hanging around for this garden party instead of rushing upstairs to shag. Everyone went to a lot of trouble to organize this."

"Now it's an engagement party."

With everyone watching us, I kiss Siobhan the right way. No peck on the lips. We kiss passionately, and everyone starts clapping and carrying on again. Just as we separate our lips, I open my eyes and see Rick shoving two fingers into his mouth to whistle.

For an hour, we mingle with our guests. My mother commandeers Siobhan for a full fifteen minutes. During one of the few stretches when I get to talk to my fiancée, we're interrupted by Bennett Montague. Not that we mind. My fiancée has told me several times today that she thinks Ben is "such a hot little sweetie-pie." There's no point in telling her he's not small. Ben is an average-size man.

The males of the species can never hope to understand the females.

When Bennett approaches us, Siobhan smiles at him. "So, Ben, when do I get to hear your secret? You said you'd tell me, eventually. This feels like that eventual moment."

No man can resist Siobhan Griffin when she's smiling.

"Oh, that," Ben says, staring down at the grass and hunching his shoulders. "It's not a secret, but I don't usually tell anyone when I first meet them. They don't really understand."

My fiancée touches his arm. "I'm very understanding."

"She honestly is," I say. "If Siobhan can overlook all my flaws, you know she'll be fine with learning the truth about you. But I've never understood why you act like it's a terrible secret. Women love it."

"A sexy secret?" Siobhan says. "Ooh, you have to tell me now."

Ben exhales a gusty breath, lifts his head, and winces. "I am Bennett Worthington Montague, crown prince of Mithoria."

"Prince?" Siobhan's eyes get even wider, then she grins and pushes her fist into Ben's chest. "You're pulling my leg."

"He's not," I say. "It's true. My employee is a prince."

"Seriously? I've never heard of Mithoria."

Ben groans. "No one has. It's a tiny country on a tiny island. But I'm also British since I have dual citizenship. I was born in the UK and went to boarding school and university here."

"You'll need to tell me all about your life as a prince."

"Not anytime soon. I have to leave this evening." He sighs, and his shoulders collapse. "Mother has summoned me. It's time for another round of 'find Ben a princess to marry,' and you know how she gets about that."

"Ah, yes," I say. "How long will you be gone this time?"

"No idea." He grimaces and scratches the back of his head. "Sorry to run out on you like this. I'd much rather stay here and do my job. Hopefully, I'll be back for Christmas."

"Your job will wait for you. Go, do your princely duty."

Ben wanders off to talk to the Dixon brothers, and I know they'll cheer him up.

As for me… The second the party breaks up, I spirit my fiancée away to our bedroom, and we have our own party in private. Afterward, I ask her the question I never got the chance to ask during the backyard celebration.

"What will you do now that you're unemployed?"

"Don't know. But I'll figure something out." She's lying on top of me, drawing invisible patterns on my chest with her finger. "I majored in math, but I minored in computer science. Maybe I could do something that uses all my skills, not just my math expertise."

"I have no doubts you will find the perfect job. Any employer would be lucky to hire you, and I'm sure you'll find something fast."

As it turns out, we're both right. Siobhan finds a job quickly, and it's one that makes use of all her expertise. My mate Grey Dixon hires her. He works as a business intelligence analyst, which involves lots of boring computer stuff and plenty of mathematical rubbish too. Maybe that's not my dream job, but I know Siobhan is over the moon about it. Grey wants to make her his official partner, legally, but she convinces him to wait so they can both make sure she's the right fit for the job.

What happened to the woman who started that rumor about me? Lady Prescott has moved to Mallorca with her lover. Lord Geoffrey, Georgina's husband, has filed for divorce, and I hear he's determined to hold on to all their assets. Apparently, I wasn't the first man Georgina propositioned, though I might be the only one who didn't accept her offer.

Who cares about the Prescotts? Siobhan and I will get married in five weeks.

And as for Bennett… Well, I hear the American Wives Club have convened an emergency meeting.

Heaven help us all.

Want more of Bennett Montague? Experience his story in *One Hot Christmas* (Hot Brits, Book 6).

Love the

Hot Brits

series?

Visit
AnnaDurand.com

to subscribe to her newsletter
for updates on forthcoming books in this series
&
to receive a free gift for signing up!

Anna Durand is a bestselling, multi-award-winning author of contemporary and paranormal romance. Her books have earned bestseller status on every major retailer and wonderful reviews from readers around the world. But that's the boring spiel. Here are the really cool things you want to know about Anna!

Born on Lackland Air Force Base in Texas, Anna grew up moving here, there, and everywhere thanks to her dad's job as an instructor pilot. She's lived in Texas (twice), Mississippi, California (twice), Michigan (twice), and Alaska—and now Ohio.

As for her writing, Anna has always made up stories in her head, but she didn't write them down until her teen years. Those first awful books went into the trash can a few years later, though she learned a lot from those stories. Eventually, she would pen her first romance novel, the paranormal romance *Willpower*, and she's never looked back since.

Want even more details about Anna? Get access to her extended bio when you subscribe to her newsletter and download the free bonus ebook, *Hot Scots Confidential*. You'll also get hot deleted scenes, character interviews, fun facts, and more! Plus you'll receive the short story *Tempted by a Kiss*, and audio bonus content narrated by Shane East, Vanessa Edwin, and Ava Lucas.

Visit AnnaDurand.com to sign up.

9 781949 406559